THE RIFT

A Family's Struggle with Political Extremism

Jamie Krell

Copyright © 2024 by Jamie Krell

2nd Edition

All rights reserved. No part of this book may be used or reproduced in any form without written permission except for brief quotations in critical articles or reviews.

Printed in the United Kingdom

For more information or to book an event, contact:

Email: jamiekrell@outlook.com

ISBN - Paperback: 9798322251255

Book formatting:

Junaid Siddique: Chjunaidsiddique2@gmail.com

Prologue

America is known as the land of the free, the land of opportunity, the land of democracy. For centuries, democracy has been the heartbeat of America. The Constitution enshrined the principles of democracy, forming the bedrock upon which American society has been built for over two centuries.

From its inception, democracy has been a guiding light for Americans. It has been the driving force behind the development of this great nation. It has been the catalyst for change, progress, and hope. The idea that individuals hold the power to select their leaders and shape their destiny is potent and sets America apart from other nations.

Throughout history, the United States has upheld democracy. Yet, there have been moments when the nation faced challenges to these democratic values. From the abolition of slavery and the Civil Rights movement to the Women's Suffrage movement and the fight for LGBTQ+ rights, Americans have consistently affirmed their beliefs. They harnessed the power of democracy to effect positive change, amplify their voices, and create a better future for everyone.

The presidents of both parties have embodied this concept of democracy. From George Washington to Abraham Lincoln, Franklin D. Roosevelt to John F. Kennedy, and Ronald Reagan to Barack Obama, presidents have always respected the mandate of the American people. They have recognised that their role is to govern and serve and that democracy is not about power but responsibility.

The President of the United States is often referred to as the leader of the free world, and this title carries significant weight. The saying "if America sneezes, the world catches a cold" highlights the idea that the United States, as an essential economic and political power, has a profound influence on the global stage. Any substantial problem or crisis within the United States has far-reaching implications for the global economy and political landscape.

This global impact is evident in the growing trend of political figures globally challenging electoral results. For example, in Brazil, populist President Jair Bolsonaro consistently cast doubt on the electoral process and refused to accept the 2021 election results. In that election, former president Lula da Silva from the left-of-centre Workers' Party narrowly defeated the incumbent with a slim margin of 50.9%. This situation mirrors the aftermath of the January 6th insurrection, where approximately 2,000 Bolsonaro supporters stormed the Supreme Federal Court, the National Congress building and the Planalto Presidential Palace in the Praça dos Três Poderes, seeking to violently overthrow the democratically elected President Lula, fuelled by unfounded allegations of electoral fraud and corruption.

The ripple effect of these events demonstrates how events in the United States can resonate worldwide, influencing political landscapes and public confidence in electoral processes. This highlights the crucial need to uphold democratic principles and honour the outcomes of free and fair elections.

Before 2020, the President of the United States symbolised the core ideals of democracy, freedom, and justice. They were the embodiment of the hopes and aspirations not only of the American people but also of individuals around the world. This profound responsibility could not be taken lightly, demanding the utmost respect, honour, and integrity.

America has frequently been described as a 'city upon a hill' and a "beacon of democracy," proudly asserting that its political system was ingeniously designed to safeguard democracy and freedom from its very inception. However, amid deep-seated divisions in contemporary America and concerns regarding the integrity of the U.S. voting system, democracy in America now finds itself in a particularly fragile state.

Indeed, the nature of democracy in America is intricately linked to the deep divisions that have long characterised the nations. The United States is a vast and diverse land, with people from all levels of society holding various beliefs and values. Yet, the democratic system that governs the country is designed to ensure that all voices are listened to, with all perspectives considered. This conflict between diversity and unity makes American democracy complex, challenging, and conflict-ridden.

Since its inception, the United States has been a melting pot of different perspectives and views, a hallmark of democracy. However, with this diversity, there are inevitable disagreements and divisions. Notwithstanding the shared values that unite Americans, such as the belief in individual liberty and the pursuit of happiness, the country has been plagued with political strife and ideological polarisation. This is the inherent nature of democracy - a system of governance where differing opinions are allowed to be shared and compete.

The Civil War was one of the most impactful events in American history, fought over the issues of slavery and states' rights. It pitted the industrialised and anti-slavery North against the agrarian and proslavery South, resulting in the loss of hundreds of thousands of lives and leaving a lasting scar on the American psyche.

In the years that followed, the country saw a series of social and political movements that further highlighted the split between different fractions of America. For example, the Civil Rights movement of the 1950s and 1960s sought to end racial segregation and discrimination but met fierce resistance from some white Americans who felt threatened by the changing social order. Similarly, the Women's Rights movement of the 1970s was met with opposition from those who believed that traditional gender roles should be upheld.

Today, America is increasingly grappling with a deep divide that threatens the stability of its democracy. Political polarisation has reached new heights, with many Americans living in two different countries. The roots of this division are complex and multifaceted, but they can be traced back to several factors.

A significant factor influencing the current political landscape is the nation's ageing population. In recent decades, the United States has experienced a noteworthy demographic shift, marked by a rising presence of individuals from diverse ethnic backgrounds, immigrants, and an expanding

LGBTQ+ community. This shift, deviating from historical norms, has triggered reactions from specific segments of the population, particularly conservative groups who perceive these changes as a challenge to their conventional way of life.

Another factor contributing to the political divide is the increasing economic inequality in the country. While the economy has boomed for some in recent years, many working-class Americans have struggled to make ends meet. This has led to frustration and anger among those left behind by the political establishment; nowhere can this be seen more than the divide between rural and urban America.

The division in America has been along not only political lines but also urban and rural lines. In recent years, the Democratic Party has lost support in rural working-class America. At the same time, the Republican Party has struggled to maintain a foothold in large urban areas. This has further fuelled the divide in America as each party becomes more entrenched in their respective regions.

Historically, the divide in America has been present since the nation's founding. The country was formed by a diverse group of people, and the question of how to balance the needs and desires of each group has been a constant challenge. Over time, these divisions have grown more profound as the country has become more diverse and the issues more complex.

Historically, in the 19th century, the United States grappled with a profound divide along regional lines, as the North and South clashed over contentious issues like slavery and states' rights. This culminated in the Civil War, which fought to resolve these issues and bring the country back together. However, the scars of the war ran deep, and the country remained divided along racial lines for many years. In the 20th century, the divide shifted to economic issues as the country struggled with the Great Depression and the Cold War. The rise of the Labour movement and the growth of the middle class helped bridge some of these divides. Still, the country remained divided over taxes, government regulation, and social welfare programs.

In recent years, a pronounced divide has surfaced—an enduring clash of ideologies often termed the "culture war." This ongoing confrontation, extending beyond America to a lesser extent in other Western nations, has spawned a relentless battle of ideas, fostering bitterness and division among the populace. The relentless struggle for supremacy plays out in nearly every facet of life, whether conservatives uphold traditional ideals or liberals advocate for sweeping change. This intensification is fuelled by the surge of social media and the ceaseless news cycle, facilitating individuals to remain entrenched within their ideological bubbles and vilify those with opposing views.

In this environment, people are now even more entrenched in their echo chambers, reinforcing their perspectives and becoming quick to vilify and dismiss anyone who doesn't perfectly align with their worldview. This toxic atmosphere has transformed political discourse into a noxious circus where insults, virtue signalling, and identity politics take centre stage. The culture war has evolved into a lucrative industry for media outlets like Fox News. With the assistance of provocative figures such as Tucker Carlson and Sean Hannity, these outlets have stoked sensationalism and disseminated misinformation on topics ranging from transgender rights to dangerous conspiracy theories regarding vaccines and the World Economic Forum. The sole aim of these channels is to profit from the discord within a deeply divided society.

The culture war and this ideological divide can be seen as one of the main reasons the two major political parties have become increasingly polarised. The Republican Party under Trump has moved further to the right, cemented more since the overturning of Roe v Wade, which has stripped millions of women of the right to abortion. Meanwhile, the Democrats have moved further to the left, with progressives such as Bernie Sanders, Alexander Ocasio Cortez, and Elizabeth Warren having more influence on the direction of the Democratic party. This has made it harder for politicians to find common ground. It is rare to work across the aisle, with legislation often relying on the so-called kingmaker, usually a moderate or independent, such as Joe Manchin or Kyrsten Sinema. The inertia of Congress has only further fuelled the divisiveness in America.

Joe Biden's winning the presidency was anticipated to mark a return to ordinary and seemingly dull politics. After four years of tumultuous and divisive governance, Biden's calm and measured demeanour promised a departure from the sensationalism and chaos that had come to define the political landscape. With his decades of experience in public service, Biden embodied the quintessential establishment figure, offering a sense of stability and familiarity, starkly contrasting with Donald Trump's presidency, marked by an unconventional and often chaotic approach.

Trump's unfiltered and combative communication style made headlines and dominated public discourse throughout his tenure, usually through tweets. His presidency was characterised by controversial policy decisions, frequent clashes with the media and political opponents, and unprecedented turnover within his administration. Trump's approach to governance disregarded historical and established norms and conventions, challenging and, in hindsight, breaking the traditional way of doing things, placing American democracy in an unstable and unprecedented place.

In the days following Joe Biden's victory, Donald Trump's response was marked by his refusal to accept the election results and his insistence on perpetuating unfounded claims of widespread voter fraud. Despite numerous court rulings and certifications by election officials, Trump persistently spread baseless conspiracy theories and actively worked to undermine the legitimacy of Biden's win. He used a barrage of tweets, public statements, and legal challenges to cast doubt on the integrity of the electoral process, ultimately fostering division and exacerbating the frustrations of his devoted supporters.

It is important to note that these false accusations were a deliberate attack on democracy. Even before the votes were cast, Trump sowed the seeds of scepticism by repeatedly suggesting that the election would be rigged against him. These baseless claims gained traction among his ardent supporters, who were primed to believe any narrative undermining the results' legitimacy. Following his defeat, Trump doubled on his false assertions, perpetuating the myth that widespread voter fraud had cost him the presidency. Despite numerous court rulings and investigations affirming the integrity of the election, Trump's persistent false claims have poisoned the well of public trust and fuelled a dangerous narrative of a stolen election. The impact of these unfounded allegations has far-reaching consequences, eroding faith in the electoral process and threatening the stability of American democracy itself.

This led to the unprecedented events of January 6th, when a violent mob of Trump supporters stormed the Capitol building to overturn the election results. The aftermath of January 6th has only served to deepen the divisions in America. The country is now more polarised than ever, with many Americans feeling that their voices are not heard and their values are not respected. The ongoing debates over racial justice, immigration, and economic inequality have only exacerbated these divisions. The world watched in horror as a mob of supporters of then-President Donald Trump stormed the U.S. Capitol building.

This insurrection, fuelled by unfounded election fraud claims, attacked the U.S. Capitol building and the very principles of democracy itself.

The aftermath of January 6th's violent attack on the Capitol revealed a deepening divide in America, with some MAGA Republicans continuing to undermine President Biden's legitimacy. By spreading baseless claims of election fraud, they erode trust in democratic institutions and perpetuate polarisation. This sustained assault on democracy hampers progress on critical issues and threatens the very essence of American governance. To safeguard democracy, it is essential for all citizens to critically assess information and engage in respectful dialogue to bridge divides and rebuild unity.

Our tale unfolds within the idyllic confines of Pine Wood, a small rural town nestled in the serene embrace of Wyoming County, New York. Against this backdrop of breathtaking natural beauty, we encounter an ordinary family entangled in the heart of a nation's turmoil, serving as a microcosm of the deep-seated fractures afflicting society.

Once inseparable, two siblings find themselves on opposite ends of an unfathomable ideological rift. Jenna, whose pursuit of higher education and newfound political awareness has fuelled her unwavering embrace of progressive liberalism, is driven by an unyielding passion for equality and social justice. On the other hand, Tyler, a once-promising and naturally intelligent individual, bears the burden of a harrowing loss that ripped through the very fabric of his being, leading him down a treacherous path. His shattered aspirations have left him susceptible to the siren song of extremist ideologies, aligning himself with the fringes of far-right beliefs.

As their journeys diverge, the fragile connections that once tightly united them now teeter on the brink of irreparable rupture. The once harmonious symphony of shared childhood memories transforms into a discordance fuelled by conflicting ideologies. Yet, these ideologies are not mere differences in opinion; they represent opposing notions of right and wrong. Their perspectives embody the antithesis of their siblings' beliefs, with such vast disparities that their outlooks on life couldn't be more divergent.

We must examine the delicate interplay between individual experiences and external influences within this complex web of divergent ideologies. Life's joys and sorrows, alongside the persuasive sway of media narratives, intertwine to shape the convictions that define our protagonists. The dichotomy between Jenna's awakening to systemic injustices and Tyler's descent into the rabbit hole of extremist doctrines invites introspection on the profound impact of circumstance and perspective.

As their lives intertwined while the larger narratives unfolded in Washington, we witnessed the choices that have indelibly shaped them as people and their beliefs. Through these experiences, further influenced by the omnipresence of media, their views have been moulded, and their perceptions of reality have been distorted. In the prescient words of Voltaire, "If you can get someone to believe absurdities, you can make them commit atrocities," stressing the dangerous power of manipulation in shaping the course of human actions. We look at the consequences on a human level at years of increasing tension in America and how it can affect ordinary people.

Chapter 1

January 6th, 2021 (Jenna's Perspective)

---※---

The January sun reflected its golden rays over a cold Pine Wood, our picturesque town in the heart of nature in Clinton County, New York state. Pine Wood is our little oasis, far from the hustle and bustle of the big cities. It is near the stunning Adirondack Park, with its rugged peaks and lush green valleys. The soft tweets of birdsong filled the air, their joyful tunes harmonising with the gentle rustling of leaves. From our cosy kitchen, where the comforting aroma of coffee and bacon dipped through the chilly winter air, I observed the familiar sights and sounds that accompanied the beginning of a new day.

Matthew, my devoted husband of 14 years, stood by the stove with a peaceful focus, attempting to flip pancakes on the hob. The sunlight filtered through the kitchen blinds, casting a warm glow upon his brownish-grey hair and highlighting the subtle lines etched upon his face, reflecting the years we had shared. His commitment to providing for our family reflected the strength and dedication he has demonstrated in every aspect of our lives.

Seated at the kitchen table, I found solace in the piles of papers sprawled across the kitchen table, a sign of my sometimes thankless yet rewarding role as a history teacher. A job I appreciate and adore so much, however, knowing that my influence extends beyond the classroom wall. In a world with so much misinformation and an era where misinformation and negative influences are prevalent on platforms such as TikTok and other social media, grasping the situation becomes truly challenging. As I observe the repercussions of these harmful influences on young and impressionable minds during everyday interactions on the playground, my responsibility as a teacher can often feel overwhelming, akin to an uphill battle.

Chapter 2 Down the Rabbit Hole

With a pen and a cup of hot coffee, I attempt to finish some last-minute marking. The marking is not due until next week, but I want to give my students more time to assess the feedback and revise and prepare for the next exam. It's more effort, but I want to give my students the best opportunity to achieve their goals.

In the background, the bustling symphony of our morning routine plays out, the clatter of utensils against countertops blended harmoniously with the sizzle of bacon cooking in the pan, creating a rhythmic backdrop to the soft scratching of my pen hitting the papers. The low buzz of the morning news emanated from the nearby television. The lively exchanges around our breakfast accompanied this constant but ambient presence.

Matthew's look held a sense of warmth and tenderness as it intersected with mine, forming an unspoken link beyond language. In that brief yet significant moment, I felt his devotion to our family's welfare and unquestionable loyalty. Without uttering a sound, it affirmed the enduring connection we'd built through years of shared dreams and responsibilities.

As partners, we successfully embarked on a delicate choreography, navigating the intricate dance of synchronising our professional ambitions, parental duties, and the everyday complexities that adorned the tapestry of our lives. This detailed dance demonstrated resolute trust, open channels of communication, and a deep understanding of each other's desires and visions. Our grand plans were driven by an unwavering determination to forge unique career paths and positively impact the world. Simultaneously, we aspired to build a loving family unit where love, family, and friends held significant importance.

Matthew and I have consistently shared a matching mindset regarding our children's upbringing. Our fundamental values of open-mindedness, empathy, and affection have shaped our parenting approach. We encouraged our children to discover who they are and their place in this confusing world around them. Our children must feel comfortable coming to us about anything and sharing any concerns or questions their young minds might have. In times of hardship, I always find joy in knowing that Matthew and I are united, prepared to confront any obstacle that life may throw at us with the same unwavering resolve and a shared parental philosophy that has shaped our journey together.

As the sweet scent of maple syrup filled the air, Matthew skilfully plated a stack of golden pancakes,

Chapter 2 Down the Rabbit Hole

their fluffy texture an invitation to gather and indulge in the delights of a shared family meal. We gathered at the table, the clatter of utensils filling the air as I celebrated the small moments like this. There was a palpable sense of enthusiasm and energy for the day ahead.

My gaze remained fixed on the window, captivated by the innate sight of Pine Wood's scenery. The presence of my family enriched me, bringing a sense of contentment to our familiar morning rituals. As we embraced our customary routine, a new day brimming with potential unfurled. Amidst the harmonious rhythm of our family's morning activities, the dulcet tunes of chirping birds intertwined with the irresistible scent of breakfast, painting a serene ambience.

Across the breakfast table are our three beautiful children patiently waiting for breakfast. There was a palpable sense of enthusiasm and energy for the day ahead. I packed my papers and pens, and my thoughts and attention shifted to our three beloved children. Lily, Gabriel, and Mia, each with their unique personalities and dreams, each at various stages of their childhood, with the world at their fingertips.

Our oldest, Lily, a thoughtful and imaginative twelve-year-old, has wisdom beyond her years, with my mother stating she was exactly like her when she was her age. Her vibrant red hair flowed like a fiery flow down her shoulders. It contrasted her calm and quiet personality, framing a face that mirrored her creative spirit. With a book in her hand, she embarked on a journey to different worlds, losing herself in the sensation of storytelling. She certainly doesn't get the imagination from Matthew or me; I can see elements of my late Mum Jean in Lily.

Gabriel, our mischievous ten-year-old, possessed a flicker in his hazel eyes that hinted at countless adventures yet to be had. His infectious laughter filled our home with buoyant energy, a reminder to embrace life's simple joys. Gabriel's curiosity knew no bounds, and his boundless energy led him on countless escapades, which could be tiring. Gabriel was also remarkably impressionable. The world around him easily influences his malleable nature.

With his mischievous spirit, he frequently sought companionship in communal activities, relishing shared experiences. He was known for his social nature, finding joy in the constant chatter and interaction with others. He exuded boundless energy and an outgoing demeanour. We valued Gabriel's individuality, understanding that his inclination

Chapter 2 Down the Rabbit Hole

towards independence and reflection were integral to his identity. I knew Gabriel would go down a unique path.

I watched my playful son at the breakfast table, a mischievous twinkle in his eyes. With his hands shaped like imaginary shooters, he aimed at his giggling sisters, Lily and Mia, who erupted into fits of laughter as his pretend shots "hit" them. As I observed this tender moment, a gentle smile played on my lips, torn between reprimanding his antics and relishing the innocence of sibling bonding. With a motherly tone that carried affection and authority, I gently said, "Gabriel, sweetheart, let's put the shooting games aside for now and enjoy our breakfast together. Lily and Mia need their brother's help finishing their pancakes!"

A mischievous moment took a turn as Gabriel, in a playful jest, shot me with an imaginary "zing." Zany laughter echoed through the room, and he returned to his breakfast, crunching and slurping cereal with carefree abandonment. I exchanged a knowing glance with my husband Matthew, pondering aloud, "I wonder why he's so drawn to these shooting games. In my day, things seemed gentler." Matthew chuckled in good humour, his eyes sparkling, and replied, "It's probably the influence of video games, my dear. Just boys being boys, nothing to worry about."

Mia, our bright-eyed seven-year-old, embodied the innocence and wonder that only a young child could possess. Mia was quite the chatterbox, always having something to ask or say. Mia had an insatiable thirst for knowledge, and her innocent questions often led to profound conversations that opened our minds and touched our hearts. Her infectious giggles could melt even the coldest of hearts.

Gathered around the kitchen table, the cadence of their voices creating a symphony of lively discussions, a profound sense of fulfilment washed over me. The life I had painstakingly constructed and the children I had lovingly nurtured all converged in this moment. It was as if the dreams I had woven into my childhood had been beyond my expectations. Their laughter and exuberance evoked the room with vibrant strokes, elevating our mornings from mere routines to moments that produced an ineffable affection and closeness that elevated the ordinary into the extraordinary.

Despite my joy, there was a lingering tinge of concern, a constant thought at the back of my mind. A murmur of unease tiptoed through my thoughts as I could hear signs of life coming from the other side of

Chapter 2 Down the Rabbit Hole

the house. Tyler, my younger 35-year-old brother, had sought refuge in our home for the last eight months, finding solace in the confines of our garage. His journey through life has had its challenges and is marked by hardships. My brother has changed over the last few years; we have become more distant, and he appears different from the person I grew up with. I believe he may lack a sense of belonging and stability and may be slightly jealous of the family I have built.

While I listened to his pain and understood the turbulent path that had brought him to our doorstep and, more specifically, a bed in the garage, I couldn't overlook the subtle tension and negativity that always seemed to arise from his presence. His scepticism and resistance to almost anything and everything put a strain on the household. Tyler's often confrontational opinions and narrow-minded view of the world often clashed with mine and Matthews and went against the values we sought to instil in our children.

Matthew, too, had expressed his concerns, worried that Tyler's influence might hinder the growth and development of our impressionable young children. Arguments were rare before Tyler entered our household. My and Matthew's personalities used to harmonise perfectly.

We'd both know each other's needs and how to overcome issues without escalating them to tension;

we were usually good at communicating issues. However, Matthew, a normally calm, happy-go-lucky and, most importantly, empathic individual, can't hide his dislike of my brother. I find it quite challenging. I know Tyler can be quite a character and even a handful at times, but I am his sister, and I can't let him down. Despite being younger, I feel I needed to somewhat Mother Tyler, especially now that our Mum has passed, given his problematic relationship with our dad.

Tyler and our dad had a tumultuous relationship marked by frequent clashes and poor communication. They often disagreed on various issues, especially personal choices like not attending college, and their arguments created tension. Their inability to communicate effectively intensified their conflicts.

Additionally, our father appeared emotionally distant, especially towards Tyler. I was always seen as his princess, which unintentionally hurt Tyler, making it difficult for him to connect with our father on a deeper level. This emotional barrier hindered their understanding of each other's perspectives and needs, ultimately straining their relationship.

Guilt was constantly tugging at my heartstrings as I grappled with the complexities of our family bond. I wanted to give Tyler the support and understanding he desperately needed. As children, we were a close-knit family; Tyler and I had many happy memories, and I knew he always had my back. Despite being my younger brother in our childhood, he often came to my rescue when approached by bullies. Nevertheless, I also felt the weight of responsibility as a mother and protector of my three children's well-being. Pursuing this delicate balancing act between a good mother and a good sister proved challenging, a continuous effort in progress. The notion that helping Tyler find stability could lead to an overall improvement lingered in my thoughts. I just knew it wasn't straightforward.

Standing by the frost-covered window, Matthew, dressed in his faded plaid shirt and smart black jeans, watched TV at the table while sipping his coffee. His gaze was reflected on the morning news playing on the television, a silent observer of the world beyond our cosy place. The news anchors spoke of the upcoming Electoral College vote count, presenting it as just another routine procedure in the democratic process. Little did we know that this day would soon be etched in history for reasons far more tumultuous than we could have imagined.

Lily, Gabriel, and Mia, now finishing breakfast, were engaged in a lively conversation, their voices

The Rift: A Family's Struggle with Political Extremism

rising and falling like a symphony of innocence and wonder. With her book tucked under her arm, Lily shared snippets of the story she had been lost in, her words painting vivid images that sparked the imagination of her younger siblings. Gabriel's hazel eyes dancing with mischief added playful embellishments to her tales, creating a world of adventure and fantasy that transported us all. Mia, her eyes shining with curiosity, absorbed every word, her tiny hands gesturing as she animatedly chimed in with her imaginative ideas.

As the morning evolved, a subtle change began to ripple through the air. The familiar footsteps approaching the house hinted at the imminent arrival of a disruptive force that would shatter the tranquillity we had carefully cultivated. Suddenly, the kitchen door swung open with a loud creak, and Tyler, my younger brother, made his boisterous entrance.

"Holy crap! It feels like I'm stuck in a fucking frozen wasteland!" Tyler's voice echoed through the house, filled with enthusiasm and a touch of exasperation. He shook off the remnants of the chilly winter air, bringing a gust of wind and a whirlwind of emotions with him.

Chapter 2 Down the Rabbit Hole

Dressed in a faded wife beater and stained jogger grey shorts, Tyler's appearance reflected the turbulence of his recent years. His messy hair and tired eyes held the weight of a troubled past, a history that had shaped his journey and left its mark on his soul. Yet, beneath the rough exterior, I still saw glimpses of the brother I had known and loved—the one who had protected me, shared secret childhood adventures, and brought laughter to our lives.

Tyler's entrance disrupted the peace that had engulfed our kitchen. The lively conversation quieted as all eyes turned to him, curiosity mingled with a hint of apprehension. Matthew glanced up from the television, his brow furrowing as he assessed the energy Tyler had brought with him. Matthew, clearly unimpressed, said, Tyler, can you watch your language?

Unfazed by the sudden attention, Tyler strolled to the kitchen counter, filling the room with anticipation and unease. He reached for an orange juice carton, his movements quick and confident, before grabbing the remote control and changing the channel to a familiar news network known for its, let's say, "conservative viewpoints". However, latterly, it became more known for peddling alt-right conspiracy theories. The room filled with the unmistakable voice of a commentator, spewing opinions and stirring the pot of political discourse.

"Why are you watching that CNN woke content? You need to wake up, Jenna! Progressive liberal propaganda is brainwashing you," Tyler's words were tinged with frustration, his eyes narrowing as he challenged the perspectives that had become our norm.

I sighed quietly, knowing that a heated debate was bound to follow. Tyler's scepticism towards mainstream media, his strong belief in conspiracy theories, and his tendency to dismiss almost everything as part of a conspiracy had become quite noticeable and draining.

Nothing is as it seems; there's always a greater enemy, and these beliefs have created an ever-widening split between us. All the same, he is my brother, but this has created a delicate balance we had strived to maintain as a family, now teetered on the edge, threatening to crumble under ideological differences.

Matthew and I exchanged glances, both of us tired of Tyler's attempts to get a reaction from us both, the unspoken tension hanging heavily in the air. Matthew couldn't hide his annoyance. His face tensed up, and he rolled his eyes; I could tell he was biting

Chapter 2 Down the Rabbit Hole

his tongue. His concern mirrored my own, a shared recognition of Tyler's influence on Gabriel, our impressionable middle child. I couldn't bear to see my children caught in the crossfire, their innocent minds entangled in a web of half-truths and misinformation.

At that moment, a surge of guilt washed over me. While I empathise with Tyler's pain and hardships, the weight of his turbulent past, and the losses he had suffered, I couldn't ignore the potential harm his influence could inflict on our children. The synchronisation we had strived to cultivate within our family was now at risk, and I couldn't help but question our choices.

Matthew, his voice filled with concern, addressed the elephant in the room. "Tyler, we've talked about this... We don't want you preaching your unusual beliefs. You know Gabriel looks up to you, and your beliefs can be divisive and, at times, appalling. We want our household to be peaceful. I can't have my children repeating some of your fucked up ideas."

Tyler's eyes darted around the room, a mix of frustration, bemusement, and defiance etched on his face. He dismissed Matthew's words with a casual wave, the tension between them palpable. It was evident that Tyler was trying to keep his thoughts to himself; I could see a smirk before he averted his gaze.

The kitchen fell silent, but our unspoken thoughts spoke volumes. It was a clash of beliefs, two different worlds coming together, and our children caught in the middle. I felt torn between my affection for my brother and my duty to protect my children. The delicate peace we had maintained seemed unstable, risking family discord.

As Matthew's departure drew near, a palpable unease settled within the walls of our home. Once warm and inviting, morning sunlight now cast elongated shadows that mirrored the conflicting emotions swirling inside me. The anticipation of Matthew's 3-day business trip to Washington, DC, mingled with the tension that had thickened the air, threatening to suffocate the fragile harmony we had carefully cultivated.

With a heavy heart, I watched as Matthew leaned down to kiss Lily, Gabriel, and Mia goodbye. Their innocent faces, filled with love and excitement, masked the turmoil coursing through our family. I yearned for a moment of respite, a fleeting escape from the mounting discord gripping us.

Tyler deliberately criticised the concept of climate change, believing it would irritate Matthew,

Chapter 2 Down the Rabbit Hole

whose zeal for environmental progress sparked Tyler's scepticism. This clash erected an invisible barrier between them, jeopardising the delicate harmony we had worked so hard to establish.

Tyler's intentions were clear – he aimed to elicit a reaction from Matthew. It was particularly significant as Matthew was about to embark on a business trip to the Climate Change Technologies Conference (CTCC), a summit highlighting innovative technologies from tech companies across North America contributing to the pursuit of net-zero emissions and green energy solutions.

My heart sank as Matthew's frustration ignited; his face spoke a thousand words despite the stone-cold silence. At that moment, I realised the gravity of the divide that had emerged, a chasm threatening to ruin the family atmosphere. A clash of ideologies had taken residence in our household and our hearts.

Sensing the imminent eruption, I swiftly positioned myself between the two men, desperate to quell the rising storm. My voice, though tinged with weariness and tingling with raw emotion, cut through the tension. "Please, let's not ruin this moment with animosity," I pleaded, my eyes darting between Matthew and Tyler, searching for a glimmer of understanding. "We must find common ground; we can believe different things and still have love and respect for each other; our views don't change the fact we are family."

Matthew's eyes met mine, echoing frustration, concern, and a longing for unity. We moved to the hallway. Matthew grabbed his bag and edged closer to the door. His voice, filled with worry and fear, trembled as he expressed concern about Tyler's influence on our children and the potential distortion of their young minds.

I knew what he meant; he meant Gabriel. For all of Gabriel's traits, one negative was his impressionability. A few months ago, he asked me about inviting his Mexican friend to his party, influenced by divisive ideologies he parroted from Tyler. I reassured Gabriel, emphasising that genuine friendship should never be based on a person's background. I encouraged him to focus on his friends' good qualities, such as their kindness and support.

Explaining the concept of friendship to a 10-year-old posed quite a challenge, as, at his tender age, friendship should be about laughter and enjoying childhood. It saddened me that I had to discuss how friendship goes beyond societal boundaries with him. It was even more disheartening that this wasn't a singular occurrence.

Chapter 2 Down the Rabbit Hole

However, his words shook me up to my core. I knew this was Tyler; Gabriel would never ask a question like that without his influence. It was a moment that deeply affected me—this moment stayed with me long after our conversation ended. Knowing that my son had taken in harmful beliefs was genuinely troubling.

Despite Tyler's influence not always being perfect, there's apparent affection between Gabriel and his uncle. They bonded over backyard soccer and English Premier League matches. It's as if Gabriel holds a special place in Tyler's heart, perhaps representing the child Tyler might have wished for. This connection makes it difficult for me to separate them, especially considering Tyler's desire for children at this stage.

I refrained from discussing Gabriel's recent troubling behaviour with Matthew, partly due to my concern about the potential impact on Tyler. I feared Matthew's immediate reaction, expecting anger and disappointment. Choosing to address the situation personally, I committed to guiding our son back to empathy, love, and understanding, determined to counteract the toxic influence that had affected him.

Back in the room, deflated and disappointed, Matthew muttered, "Once I am back, we need to set strict ground rules, or he's gone." We can't risk him influencing Gabriel and his sisters; some of his narrow-minded views don't belong in modern-day America, let alone in our home". I nodded in agreement; I knew he was correct, but it was a lot to take in.

With a tender kiss, Matthew reluctantly released my hand and approached the front door, ready to embark on his trip. As he turned the doorknob, our eyes locked again, conveying a deep love between us but an awareness that some things need to change regarding Tyler.

The door closed with a firm click, signalling his departure was final. In the hallway, the moment embraced me, casting a shadow over the calm morning. Inside, a mix of feelings swirled – affection, remorse, and determination.

As I walked back towards the kitchen, drinking the last few sips of my lukewarm coffee and telling the kids we had 5 minutes before we needed to go, I mustered the courage to ask Tyler about his plans for the day. The tension between us was palpable, but I couldn't ignore it. "So, Tyler, what's on your agenda today?"

A mischievous smirk played across Tyler's face as he leaned back in his chair. "Just recording a new

Chapter 2 Down the Rabbit Hole

episode podcast for my support group," he replied calmly.

My heart sank. Despite never listening to an episode, I knew all too well what Tyler's "support group" was. It was a haven for conspiracy theories and extremist ideologies. Deep down, I felt a wave of worry wash over me, knowing the dangerous path Tyler had gone down. However, like everything with my brother, I try to repress it and hope it goes away.

Summoning my resolve, I confronted him with concern and defeatism. "You need to start thinking about getting a job, Tyler. You can't keep relying on others. Matthew is getting fed up with you constantly freeloading."

A mocking laugh escaped Tyler's lips as he rolled his eyes dismissively. "Oh, please. Like Matthew's opinion means anything, he's just another brainwashed sheep in this messed-up society; his job is a joke, and he is a slave of the woke blob."

His words stung. The disrespect he showed towards Matthew, my husband, and the father of our children crossed a line. Tyler then shouted, "What do you both not get? People like me can't get jobs; I've been replaced by cheap illegal scavengers." I put my hands over my face, recognising that I couldn't simply stand by and allow Tyler's troubling beliefs to continue affecting our family.

The Rift: A Family's Struggle with Political Extremism

The tension in the room was palpable, and I could see Lily and Gabriel, our perceptive children, watching us with concerned eyes. Gabriel's innocent curiosity got the better of him as he tugged at my sleeve. "Mum, what does 'brainwash' mean?"

A wave of stress washed over me, a clear signal that I needed to act promptly to protect them from this negative influence. In a sudden realisation, I made a spontaneous decision – it was clear that change was necessary. However, time was running out, and our work commitments awaited. "It's time to go, or we might be late for school," I said, my voice covering the concern that had come over me.

As I quickly herded the kids into the car, a mix of emotions swirled within me. I couldn't ignore the sinking feeling that Tyler was stuck down a rabbit hole of anger and resentment.

As I started the car and left our home, I felt uncertain about handling Tyler. Deep down, it was apparent he needed support and guidance. I wanted to help him so much, but I also promised to protect my loved ones from harmful influences and ideas that could harm our family.

Chapter 2

Down the Rabbit Hole (Tyler's Perspective)

Sitting alone in the faintly lit living room, the remnants of my heated exchange lingered in the air, stirring up a mix of frustration and pity within me. My sister Jenna appeared as a timid, lost soul trapped in societal brainwashing. I couldn't help but feel a twinge of disappointment for her inability to see beyond the comforting veil of mainstream narratives or question anything she said.

As I thought about our clash of beliefs, I couldn't help but feel bemused and worried about the influences these prevailing narratives would have on my innocent nieces and nephew. I feared that their minds would be moulded by the liberal elites, indoctrinating them with tales of climate change-induced doomsday scenarios and manipulating their young and impressionable emotions. I believe Matthew, Jenna's husband, was an unwitting accomplice, spreading fear and anxiety among their children with his unwavering belief in the climate change agenda.

I held no ill will towards Jenna, my sister, and I love her. I profoundly pity her inability to break free from the chains that bound her. I pitied her lack of intellectual curiosity and reluctance to venture beyond the surface-level understanding of the world. She saw my pursuit of alternative knowledge as a threat, an aberration that disturbed the delicate balance she had built around her. Compounding the situation is her condescending attitude; she believes she's superior and more intelligent than me due to her college education.

Despite our heated exchange, Jenna accused me of being a freeloader, dismissing the importance of my work. Yet, in her narrow view, she failed to grasp the significance of the battles I fought in the realm of ideas. She accepted the COVID-19 narrative and was happy to pump untested things into her

Chapter 2 Down the Rabbit Hole

body. My quest for truth and awakening appeared futile to her, a mere distraction from the conventional paths of success and stability. Still, I question where my robust baby sister went.

Jenna's failure to understand the depth of my dedication only strengthened my determination. I was motivated by an intense desire for knowledge and to uncover hidden truths most people overlooked. My quest for different viewpoints and critical analysis wasn't just an intellectual endeavour; it was a moral obligation to question the mainstream narrative and the influence of the elite over humanity.

I aimed to free minds, including Jenna's, from the grip of deception, which is why I am a leading contributor on various forums and recently set up a no-holds-bar podcast.

Jenna and I were close in our youth, and that closeness endured until recently. She used to be my rock, the older sister I'd rely on for guidance regarding dating and life decisions. I chose to do an apprenticeship in car mechanics at the local community college, a far more appealing choice than the likely alternative of working in the numerous cafes and bars in Pine Wood. These establishments are essentially the only businesses still operating in Pine Wood.

The Rift: A Family's Struggle with Political Extremism

Unlike me, my sister always appeared to have a perfectly organised life. Her accomplishments in school and college and her natural ability to captivate attention occasionally left me feeling like I was merely an afterthought.

I wasn't resentful, really. It was more like this feeling of being in her shadow. I had my quirks and energy, but they paled in comparison. Jenna was the responsible one, the one with the answers. Everything seemed to revolve around her achievements. I felt like I always thought differently. I always question everything, which would drive Mum and Dad crazy.

My late Mum would be more tolerant of my views and appreciated that I would think outside the box. I felt like my Mum understood me much more. In contrast, my relationship with my dad was vastly different. There were frequent clashes about anything and everything; fundamentally, effective communication was lacking. He disagreed with my life choices, particularly my decision not to go to college, which caused much tension.

Even prior, though, my dad always seemed emotionally distant, and it was hard for me to connect with him on a deeper level. He was usually busy, and when he had time, it often went to Jenna, which made me feel second-best the whole time. This emotional

Chapter 2 Down the Rabbit Hole

barrier kept growing, and it strained our relationship. During the last few years, when I needed him most after enduring the most challenging times of my life, he wasn't by my side, and I find it impossible to forgive him.

As the impacts of our argument faded into the room's tranquillity, I resigned myself to the fact that most people prefer to take the metaphorical blue pill rather than the more frightening red pill.

Jenna's unquestionable acceptance of mainstream narratives and liberal indoctrination shows she isn't strong enough to see the truth. Although I criticised her, my conviction remained unshaken. I believed that true enlightenment could be achieved only by confronting unfounded truths.

As I retreated to the familiar confines of the garage, my sanctuary away from the perceived conformity of the household, I prepared myself for the upcoming episode of "The Red Pill Awakening." The podcast had been gaining momentum, finding a growing audience among like-minded individuals who sought to unravel the truths concealed beneath the veil of mainstream narratives. Through this platform, we connected a network of QAnon and America First supporters united in our quest for the hidden realities that escaped the masses despite being in plain sight.

The Rift: A Family's Struggle with Political Extremism

The cluttered space reflected my tumultuous thoughts as I moved into the makeshift workstation. Cables traversed the worn desk, connecting various devices and boosting the power of our message. Posters adorned the walls, featuring enigmatic symbols and cryptic messages, serving as constant reminders of the hidden truths waiting to be unveiled.

The low lighting in the garage cast elongated shadows, heightening the sense of secrecy that enveloped our endeavour. Surrounded by the remnants of past episodes, stacks of papers filled with hastily scribbled notes and talking points for the next episode, I indulged in the fervour of preparation. The air was thick with anticipation, tinged with a heady mixture of disdain for the Clintons, Obama, and what I perceived as the liberal elite. My research is a concoction of QAnon revelations, alternative media sources, and random titbits' finding the underlying cause of things people are blinded by.

With each passing day, my conviction grew more robust. I believed I was serving society, a noble act of awakening the slumbering minds entrapped by the illusions perpetuated by the mainstream media. The relentless pursuit of truth had become my life's mission, even if it meant swimming against the tide of social acceptance.

The podcast had found its niche, resonating with the enthusiasm of QAnon supporters who sought to validate their scepticism of the established order. It became a platform where the hidden truths could be dissected and shared, offering solace to those who believed the orchestrated narratives of the ruling class marginalised them. The growing number of listeners and the messages of gratitude and solidarity reaffirmed our collective mission to break free from the shackles of deception.

As I sat in the makeshift studio, surrounded by an array of microphones, computer screens, and a jumble of cables, I took a moment to reflect on the power of our message. The thrill of being part of a movement that dared to challenge the prevailing narratives coursed through my veins. It was a rebellion against the status quo, a rallying cry for those who felt marginalised and silenced in a world dominated by liberal elites.

With the click of a mouse, the recording software came to life, ready to capture our voices and transmit them into the digital realm. I cleared my throat. My mind focused on the forthcoming monologue, a diatribe against woke culture, transgender rights, and the perceived deterioration of traditional values. It was a delicate balance, a dance on the tightrope of political correctness, where I aimed to ignite passion without crossing the line into outright hate.

As the red recording light reflected in the darkness, my thoughts turned to the disturbing truths I would unleash. The profoundly offensive rhetoric regarding migrants taking jobs, the incendiary assertions about globalist conspiracies, and the thinly veiled racism sparked certain movement areas.

A subtle internal conflict brewed within me, a collision between my relentless dedication to the cause and the hesitations stirred by Jenna's expression. She stood as a link to the world I had moved away from, a steady reminder of familial bonds I had once treasured. However, in my pursuit of truth, such connections were regarded sceptically, as they could compromise clear judgment. In all honesty, Jenna falls prey to the influences of our liberal society, shaped by the established norms.

As I prepared to unleash our podcast "The Red Pill Awakening." upon the digital landscape, my thoughts were interrupted by the crackling voice of Charlie, my best friend dating back from school and co-host, through the headphones. As Charlie was joining through Zoom, his excitement was palpable

Chapter 2 Down the Rabbit Hole

and infectious as he announced our show's growing popularity and the increasing number of young listeners who found solace in our knowing the truth.

Charlie and I have a long history dating back to our school days. While we may have started as two individuals with distinct paths, our friendship was built on shared interests and a mutual love for American sports, particularly football and baseball. We would spend hours jamming together, with Charlie on the drums and me strumming away on my guitar, creating melodies that echoed through our small town.

In those early years, politics didn't consume our conversations or shape our worldviews. We were carefree and focused on the joys of youth, bonding over our shared musical passions and the thrill of cheering on our favourite sports teams. During those moments of camaraderie, our friendship deepened as we revelled in the freedom of self-expression and the power of Music to bring people together.

Charlie had always been more vocal about his beliefs, with a firm conviction in what he saw as America's core values. His early outlook was influenced by his father, a true American patriot with strong evangelical conservative values. While I respected Charlie's unwavering dedication to his ideals, I didn't fully embrace his political views.

Politics seemed distant and disconnected from my priorities and interests.

In Charlie's eyes, his dad was a symbol of strength and patriotism, someone who stood up for what he believed in, no matter how controversial or divisive. His father's influence profoundly impacted Charlie's convictions, shaping his perspective on the world and cementing his resolve to defend what he saw as the true essence of the nation.

The snowflakes and woke mob may label Charlie's dad as a neo-Nazi, but that is nonsense. For Charlie, his dad represented the embodiment of America he admired—a country rooted in traditional values, strong borders, and an unwavering commitment to individual liberties. He saw his father as a beacon of hope, a true patriot who fought tirelessly to preserve what he believed were the core foundations of their beloved nation.

For myself, the journey was gradual. I began to question the world and prevailing narratives and became increasingly aware of what I perceived as an erosion of the typical values I held dear. A gradual awakening and self-discovery journey led me to embrace a more conservative perspective. The political landscape became relevant, and I aligned more closely with Charlie's views.

Chapter 2 Down the Rabbit Hole

Looking around me, I can't help but feel a deep discontent with the way America is changing. Everything that once made us strong and proud is slipping away. The multiculturalism touted as progress feels like it's erasing our American identity, traditions, and values. I now need to feel shame to be American and guilty for my past; it's nothing but woke, anti-American bullshit.

I yearn for the good old-fashioned American values that seem to be fading away. Hard work, personal responsibility, and a sense of community used to be the backbone of this country. It feels like we're losing touch with what made us great.

I refuse to feel guilty about being American. I believe in the principles of nationalism and traditionalism because they offer a way to preserve our heritage, our culture, and our way of life. We must prioritise our citizens and protect what's ours before we lose it completely.

And I can't ignore the creeping intrusion of the government into our lives. It's suffocating our freedom and hindering our ability to pursue our dreams. We should have the right to make our own choices without the heavy hand of the government weighing us down. The Democrats are trying to remove my right to bear arms and tell me what sort of car I should own; they are intruding into people's rights.

As Charlie and I's friendship evolved, so did our ambitions; we would no longer let snowflakes defame America. We recognised the power and ability of our voices to reach a wider audience. We then conceived the idea of "The Red Pill Awakening" podcast. On this platform, we could share our alternative perspective and challenge the prevailing narratives we believed were leading America astray.

As Charlie and I prepared to record another episode of "The Red Pill Awakening," I couldn't help but reflect on our journey. We had come a long way from our carefree days of playing Music and cheering for our sports teams. We had transformed into advocates for what we believed were the core principles that would lead America back to greatness. Most of our episode is recorded, but it's time for my opening monologue. This is my favourite bit; I can express my feelings.

[Opening Jingle]

Tyler: *"Welcome, fellow truth-seekers, to another episode of The Red Pill Awakening. Today, we're delving into a topic that the mainstream media often avoids: migrants and borders. Get ready for some unapologetic truths!*

Chapter 2 Down the Rabbit Hole

Let's start by acknowledging that our nation's borders are under siege. We're facing an unprecedented influx of migrants, flooding uninvited, burdening our resources, and compromising our national security. It's time to wake up from the politically correct slumber and confront this harsh reality.

First, we must preserve the sanctity of our borders. They're the gatekeepers to our way of life, culture, and values. Our ancestors fought tooth and nail to build this great nation, and we owe it to them to protect what they've created. It's not about hate; it's about safeguarding our identity.

The liberal elites and woke blob in Washington and Silicon Valley, with their bleeding hearts, insist on open borders and unchecked migration. But let me tell you, their naivety is dangerous. We can't be the world's charity, constantly shouldering the burden of millions seeking a free ride. It's time to prioritise our citizens, their jobs, their safety, and their welfare.

Some will label us heartless, but that's far from the truth. We believe in compassionate and controlled immigration. Those who enter our country should do so legally, respecting our laws and values. We welcome those willing to assimilate, contribute, and become productive members of our society.

But enough is enough! We can't continue to turn a blind eye to the criminal elements that exploit our porous borders. Drug cartels, human traffickers, and gangs are pouring in, wreaking havoc on our communities. It's time to deploy every resource necessary to secure our borders, whether physical barriers, increased patrols, or advanced technology.

And let's address the elephant in the room: the mainstream media's obsession with demonising anyone who dares to speak the truth. They label us racists, xenophobes, and bigots simply for daring to question the wisdom of unchecked migration. But we won't be silenced. We will continue to fight for the preservation of our nation, our culture, and our values.

So, my fellow red pillars, it's time to awaken the masses to the harsh realities surrounding migrants and borders. We must demand decisive action, stricter immigration policies, and a commitment to protecting our citizens. The future of our great nation depends on it...

More to come after this ad break."

Chapter 2 Down the Rabbit Hole

[Upbeat music playing]

Tyler: "Hey there, freedom-loving folks! Are you tired of being tracked, monitored, and treated like another data point? Well, we've got the solution for you!"

Charlie: "Introducing 'Liberty Shield VPN'—the ultimate tool to protect online privacy and reclaim digital independence. With Liberty Shield VPN, you can browse, stream, and communicate securely without Big Brother breathing down your neck."

Tyler: "That's right, Charlie! Our innovative technology encrypts your internet connection, making it virtually impossible for anyone to spy on your online activities. Say goodbye to prying eyes and hello to the freedom to explore the digital realm without fear."

Charlie: "But it doesn't stop there, folks! We've partnered with companies that value your privacy as much as ours. If you type in the promo code REDPILL, you will get 20% off your first-year subscription. They see the power of our growing audience and are thrilled to support us in our mission to protect your digital rights."

The Rift: A Family's Struggle with Political Extremism

Tyler: "By choosing Liberty Shield VPN, you're not only taking control of your online security, but you're also sending a powerful message to these companies: your privacy matters, and they are happy to contribute to our cause."

Charlie: "So join us, the defenders of digital freedom, and become part of the Liberty Shield VPN family today. Experience the peace of mind of browsing the internet on your terms. Together, we'll continue to champion privacy as a fundamental right."

Tyler: "Don't wait! Take a stand, protect your digital sovereignty, and show the world that you won't compromise when it comes to your online freedom. Get Liberty Shield VPN now and enjoy the benefits of a secure and private online experience. "

[Music fades out]

It was ironic that Liberty Shield VPN was paying us to promote them. They were just a typical morally corrupt corporation. They were chasing the money. I know they tweeted support for BLM and threw the rainbow flag in our faces on pride

Chapter 2 Down the Rabbit Hole

weekend. However, with their sponsorship money, we can grow our base and open more people's minds.

The show continued with discussions about the week's events, including a chat about trans athletes and an exploration of the current topics on Twitter and social media.

I took a moment to reflect on my journey from an unengaged and ignorant young person who would swallow the mainstream narrative.

I saw myself as a role model and truth-seeker, exposing society's lies and deceptions. I felt a sense of pride for the people. I was awakening people's minds and educating people.

Charlie: *"Welcome back to The Red Pill Awakening, your weekly dose of unfiltered truth. Now, we're diving deep into a topic that challenges the mainstream narrative—women's roles. Strap in, folks, because it's time to peel back the layers of political correctness and expose the reality hidden from us.*

First off, let's address the elephant in the room. Women have been systematically misled by the liberal agenda, which promotes this illusion of gender equality while neglecting the undeniable biological and psychological differences between men and women. It's time to embrace the truth and rediscover the beauty of traditional gender roles.

Women, it's time to embrace your true nature, your inherent femininity. Society has tried to convince you to abandon your nurturing instincts and natural inclination to care for your family and create a warm and loving home. But here's the red pill: The family unit is the bedrock of civilisation, and your role within it is crucial.

Ladies, you hold immense power and influence in shaping future generations. Embrace motherhood, cherish it, and reject the toxic idea that a career is the ultimate measure of success. Your nurturing touch and unconditional love can create strong, virtuous individuals who will go on to build a better society.

Let's face it: feminism has gone astray. It has bred resentment, division, and a toxic battle between the sexes. We must restore balance by recognising and celebrating the complementary roles of men and women. Men are natural protectors and providers, while women are the heart and soul of the family. It's time to embrace these roles again for our society's betterment.

Chapter 2 Down the Rabbit Hole

Some may accuse us of trying to suppress women's rights, but that couldn't be further from the truth. We advocate for a return to the natural order, where each gender can thrive in their respective domains. It's about honouring the unique strengths and qualities of both men and women.

So, my fellow truth-seekers, let's reject the lies of the liberal agenda and reclaim our traditional values. Let's celebrate the importance of women's roles in nurturing families, promoting stability, and cultivating a sense of purpose in the hearts of our children. Together, we can build a future that cherishes the true essence of femininity and masculinity."

Charlie's parting words reverberated through the microphone, carrying a distinct tone of sexism and derogatory comments that left an impression. My mind briefly brought up images of my sister, niece, and mother. A sense of unease tickled my conscience momentarily. Yet, it swiftly dissipated, overtaken by the enthusiasm and assurance that my efforts positively impacted the world.

Charlie, sensing my momentary pause even over Zoom, enthusiastically shared his screen, displaying the analytics for our podcast. "Take a look, Tyler," he said with a wide grin. "Our listener figures are exploding, especially among young men aged 19 to 35. We're reaching more and more people, my friend. We're making a difference."

I turned my attention to the screen, eyes scanning the numbers and graphs that portrayed our growing audience. The surge of listeners, particularly among young men, was undeniable and showed that our message was spreading. It validated that our message resonated and that we successfully applied what we believed to be the truth. The doubts that had briefly flickered within me were extinguished, replaced by a sense of purpose and determination.

A rush of exhilaration washed over me. I saw myself as a warrior for justice, fighting against what I perceived as the erosion of traditional values and the corruption of society. The thought of waking people up from their complacency and leading them toward a brighter future fuelled my convictions. The perception that I was part of something greater, part of a movement that would shape history, outweighed any lingering uncertainty.

Chapter 3

Schism (Jenna's Perspective)

I thought the car ride to school would distract me from the tension and the drama of this morning's events. While I dropped Mia off at Elementary school without any trouble, I then made my way to Gabriel's and Lily Middle School, which was, luckily, only a few miles away from the high school where I work.

Lily was no trouble; she just played on her phone with a big grin and not a worry on her mind. She was consumed in her games and singing away, which melted my heart. In contrast, I couldn't shake my heart's unease while driving Gabriel to school.

The Rift: A Family's Struggle with Political Extremism

With Tyler's increasing influence, I occasionally felt anxious about the questions he might pose; following the heated morning altercation with Tyler, it became evident that my apprehension was justified.

"Mom, why do people make such a big deal about free speech?" Gabriel's innocent voice broke the silence in the car, but his tone hinted at something naughty.

I furrowed my brows, carefully choosing my words. "Well, sweetie, free speech is important, but we also need to be responsible with our words. They can have consequences, and we should consider how they may affect others."

"But Tyler says we should be able to say whatever we want, even if it offends people," he continued, reflecting a newfound boldness.

My grip on the steering wheel shifted, and my concerns grew. "Tyler has his opinions, darling, but we must always treat others kindly and respect their feelings and beliefs. It's not about pushing boundaries with our words but about understanding and empathy."

My head was pounding as we continued our drive. Gabriel's questions took a more uncomfortable turn. "Mom, why do some people hate others just because they're different?"

Chapter 3 Schism

A twinge of sadness pierced my heart. How do I explain intolerance to my young son in a way he can grasp? "Well, honey, some people are afraid of what they don't understand, so they react with hate. But we need to embrace diversity and treat everyone with respect and empathy."

"But Tyler says some people don't belong here and that they ruin our country," Gabriel persisted.

I could feel my patience wearing thin, but I knew I needed to address his concerns with understanding. "Hey, Gabriel, it's not okay to think everyone is the same just because a few people mess up. We should try to see the good things in everyone, no matter where they're from or what they think."

Silence settled in the car as I knew I had to figure out how to talk to Gabriel without getting mad. I knew I had to have a deep conversation with him about why thinking and feeling for others is essential.

I took a deep breath and turned to him, my expression softening. "I'm sorry if I seemed upset, sweetheart. You must understand that sometimes, people can influence us with ideas that might not align with our values. Being respectful, understanding, and kind to others will always be the most important values in our family."

The Rift: A Family's Struggle with Political Extremism

I looked into his eyes, hoping my words had impacted him and planted a seed of critical thinking and empathy in his young, impressionable mind.

After I dropped Gabriel and Lily off, I drove to my high school. I had a busy day of teaching and marking. My head was pounding; the stress of this morning had really taken its toll on me as I parked in the busy car park, attempting to cherish the moments of peace.

After collecting some items from the staff room, I walked into my classroom a few minutes before the first period. Before the students arrived, I took a few moments to stand by the window, looking out at the morning sunlight spilling through the leaves of the trees. The gentle sway of branches and the soft chirping of birds provided a brief but much-needed respite from the chaos in my head.

Inhaling deeply, I reminded myself that as an educator, my role extended far beyond my subjective experiences and disagreements. I had the opportunity to shape young minds to open doors of understanding and empathy.

Ironically enough, today's lesson was on the Civil Rights Movement. This topic became increasingly important in America, which you can argue is becoming increasingly divided. The Civil

Chapter 3 Schism

Rights Movement is something close to my heart and an issue that opened my world when I enrolled at the college.

Rosa Parks and Fannie Lou Hamer have a special place in my heart for their courage and their ability to exemplify the power of individual action in the face of injustice. Fannie Lou Hamer's unwavering dedication to voting rights and resolute determination inspire me to advocate for equality and stand up for my convictions. These remarkable women epitomise the strength and resilience I aspire to embody in both my life and teaching.

I approached my desk, my fingertips brushing the familiar surface as I sought to ground myself. The burden of the earlier argument with Tyler still clung to me, causing a subtle tension in my shoulders. I closed my eyes, taking slow, deliberate breaths, consciously releasing the lingering frustration and replacing it with a renewed sense of purpose.

My students' voices filled the air as the classroom door swung open, their laughter and conversations blending into a symphony of youthful energy. With a deep breath, I straightened my posture, plastered a warm smile, and greeted each student individually as they entered the room. Their vibrant spirits and eager expressions reminded me of the potential within each of them.

The Rift: A Family's Struggle with Political Extremism

Once the students settled into their seats, the classroom hummed with anticipation. I could feel their eyes on me, awaiting the knowledge and guidance I was there to impart. I took a moment to look around the room, appreciating the diversity of faces and backgrounds. It reminded us that we could find common ground and understanding within these walls, even amidst the most challenging topics.

Gradually, the chatter died down, signalling the moment to begin. I stood before the class, my voice steady yet warm as I introduced the life and legacy of Martin Luther King Jr. I watched as their attention sharpened, their eyes fixed on me, hungry for knowledge and eager to explore the lessons of history.

With each word I spoke, I immersed myself in the stories of courage and resilience. In my head, the morning's argument began to fade into the background as I found comfort in the power of education. I believed, with unwavering conviction, that by understanding the struggles of others, we could build a better future grounded in empathy and justice.

I stood at the front of my bustling classroom, ready to embark on a thought-provoking lesson centred around the influential figure of Martin Luther

Chapter 3 Schism

King Jr. and the profound impact of the Civil Rights Movement. Excitement and anticipation filled the air as I began sharing the historical context and significance of this transformative period in American history.

As I detailed the tireless efforts of Martin Luther King Jr. to combat racial inequality and injustice, I observed a restlessness among some of my students. One student, Jacob, raised his hand tentatively, his eyes reflecting curiosity and apprehension. I welcomed his participation and encouraged him to share his thoughts.

"Um, Ms. Johnson," Jacob started, his voice quivering slightly, "I understand the importance of Martin Luther King Jr's work, but sometimes it feels like the Civil Rights Movement has gone too far. As a white person, I sometimes find myself feeling blamed for the past, for things I didn't personally do, and it makes me uncomfortable."

His vulnerability struck a chord in me. I could sense Jacob's internal struggle, grappling with complex emotions and his place in a conversation about racial equality. I nodded understandingly, acknowledging the depth of his concerns. "Jacob, thank you for your honesty. Conversations about race can be challenging, and it's important to recognise the multitude of emotions they can evoke. Our goal here is to foster understanding and empathy for one another."

Jacob, known for his outspoken nature, interjected passionately, "But Ms. Johnson, it is not fair that we, as individuals, are constantly responsible for the actions of the past. We didn't personally participate in slavery or discrimination. Why should we bear the burden of guilt?". There were murmurs of agreement from some of his fellow students.

It was a sentiment I had encountered before, born out of a sincere desire for fairness. I took a deep breath, preparing to address Jacob's concerns thoughtfully. I responded, "You both raise an important point. It is true that none of us individually caused the historical injustices of the past. Still, it's crucial to acknowledge the ongoing impact of systemic inequality. Understanding our history, confronting its complexities, and working towards a more equitable future can create a society where everyone feels valued and respected."

Our history lessons aren't about assigning blame or guilt but understanding the historical context and working together toward a more just society. True equality benefits everyone and isn't a threat, but a path to collective progress."

Chapter 3 Schism

Aisha, a normally quiet, shy student known for deep thinking, raised her hand. With a steady gaze, she spoke with a calm determination that commanded attention.

"Jacob, I understand where you're coming from. I do. But let me share a bit about my life as a Black female. I've encountered numerous instances where I've been judged not for who I am but solely based on my skin colour. Security guards have unjustifiably followed me, questioned my English proficiency, and asked about my origin. I could go on and on.

It's not about making anyone feel guilty; it's about shedding light on the injustices that still exist today. When you're accustomed to privilege, equality can sometimes feel like oppression. But it's important to remember that true equality requires acknowledging and addressing persistent inequalities."

Aisha's words hung in the air, creating a moment of profound reflection. Jacob's anger softened, and I could see a flicker of understanding in his eyes. His face completely changed, and I could see him consider the words he just heard. The room was filled with a collective sense of empathy and the realisation that our journeys were interconnected. Powerful and vital conversations erupted in the classroom, and opinions were challenged. However, respect was plenty.

Our classroom had become a microcosm of America and the wider world, where political polarisation seeped into the minds of our students, often mirroring the views they were exposed to in their communities, particularly those of their parents. It was a sobering realisation that even in the sanctuary of education, the echoes of division could be heard.

I had witnessed how easily students could fall into the trap of echo chambers, where differing opinions were dismissed or ignored, and the cycle of polarisation was perpetuated. It left me with a sense of unease, a fear that our young minds might become entangled in the web of rigid ideologies, closing themselves off to the transformative power of diverse perspectives.

These concerns became deeply personal for me as I looked at my own family, my children, and my brother Tyler's influence on them. His rigid beliefs and the extremist echo chamber he had fallen into left me bewildered and concerned. I recognised the urgent need for patience and open dialogue to bridge the growing divide within my family.

Chapter 3 Schism

Although, it was genuinely distressing to witness the inevitable repercussions of political content and culture wars from social media, particularly TikTok and Instagram, in our classroom. The constant exposure of students to these platforms made it almost unavoidable that the toxic atmosphere of division in wider society would permeate our educational sanctuary.

The profound impact of these online spaces on young minds, shaping their views and perspectives, became glaringly evident as their beliefs often mirrored the divisive narratives circulating online. The classroom, meant to be a haven for learning and growth, had morphed into a reflection of the broader societal discord.

Witnessing students easily succumb to echo chambers, where differing opinions were dismissed and the cycle of polarisation thrived, left me with a heavy heart. This realisation brings forth a deep sense of sadness, highlighting the urgent need to address the influence of social media on shaping the mindset of the younger generation and fostering an environment that promotes open-mindedness and critical thinking.

The journey that had begun with my college days, with my awakening to the issues of political polarisation, felt more relevant than ever. I embarked on this path of education and dialogue to foster understanding and break down the walls of division. As I stood there, I realised the work was far from over — instilling a sense of critical thinking and empathy in my children.

As the bell rang, signalling the end of the first period, I gathered my belongings. I walked out of the classroom, mixed emotions swirling within me. The intense discussion we had just experienced had peeled back the layers, revealing the depth to which political polarisation had infiltrated the minds of our students. It was both enlightening and disheartening, leaving me with a significant responsibility for their future.

Making my way through the bustling corridors, my attention was caught by a cluster of boys gathered closely, their focus locked onto a phone. Driven by curiosity, I moved forward, compelled to explore what had seized their interest enough to make a small crowd gather behind them.

As I moved the distance, my heart sank as I saw the video podcast playing on the screen. It was an interview featuring an infamous figure, a leader of the far-right group "American First." The screen was filled with vile and hateful rhetoric, spewing ideas of the "great replacement theory" and calling for

Chapter 3 Schism

revolutionary actions. The dangerous ideology being broadcasted made my stomach churn with anger and despair.

And then, the unthinkable realisation struck me like a lightning bolt— the person being interviewed was none other than my brother, Tyler. The connection between him and these radical ideologies shook me to my core. My mind swirled with disbelief and profound concern as I grappled to understand how he had been led down such a dangerous path.

I took responsibility for the situation, urging the boys to return to their classrooms. It was crucial to reclaim their attention and steer them away from the toxic influence of the video. With a firm resolve, I retrieved the phone from their grasp, holding the device in my hands, my gaze transfixed by the screen that had ensnared my brother's mind.

I was shaking; I couldn't believe it. I knew my brother was into some unpleasant view, but not this. I feel literally sick. However, could my brother share and give a platform to such a despicable soul who believes in white supremacists? I can't quite believe my worst nightmares have become real.

Chapter 4

Adrift (Tyler's Perspective)

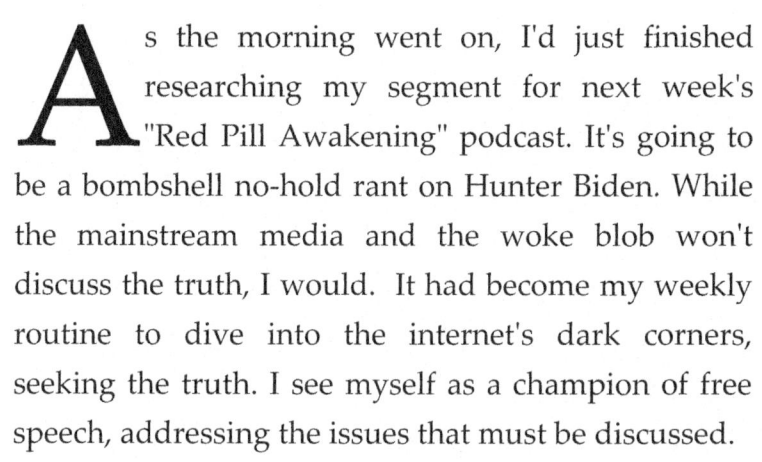

A s the morning went on, I'd just finished researching my segment for next week's "Red Pill Awakening" podcast. It's going to be a bombshell no-hold rant on Hunter Biden. While the mainstream media and the woke blob won't discuss the truth, I would. It had become my weekly routine to dive into the internet's dark corners, seeking the truth. I see myself as a champion of free speech, addressing the issues that must be discussed.

I should clarify that delving into the world of current affairs and truth-seeking was a stark departure from the person I used to be. You see, I had always been fascinated by machines and had built a successful career as a skilled mechanic. Cars and, more specifically, fixing cars were more than just a job to me; it was a passion that filled my days with purpose.

During my school summers, a close family friend recognised my passion for mechanics and provided an opportunity for me to explore it further. This experience led to completing an apprenticeship and eventually forging a career. Despite my father's objections, who hoped for a more traditional path like Jenna's, finishing high school and attending college, they didn't hide their disappointment.

I owe much of my knowledge and expertise to the skilled mechanics who mentored me during those formative years. The hours spent in that garage, absorbing every bit of knowledge and honing my skills, shaped me into the mechanic I am today. It was more than just a training ground; it was a place of friendship with down-to-earth people who shared a love for all aspects of automotive.

Speaking of automotive love, my heart beats for classic American cars. There's something magical about those timeless machines that capture my imagination. The elegance of a Ford Mustang, the raw power of a Chevrolet Camaro, the iconic presence of a Dodge Charger, and the exhilaration of a Pontiac

Chapter 4 Adrift

GTO hold a special place in my heart. Restoring and maintaining these vintage beauties felt like breathing life into history, keeping the spirit of American automotive ingenuity alive.

And let's not forget my deep-rooted passion for NASCAR. The thunderous roar of the engines, the smell of burning rubber, and the adrenaline rush as cars race inches apart—an experience like no other. NASCAR embodies the perfect fusion of speed, skill, and strategy. Cheering on my favourite drivers, witnessing the intense battles for victory, and being part of the NASCAR community is an exhilarating journey I wholeheartedly embrace. Though, like everything in my life, that all changed when tragedy struck, tearing apart the life I had known.

Laura, my childhood sweetheart and the love of my life had been studying medicine at Harvard. Our future seemed bright and full of hope; Laura and I had our future planned, from the kitchen in our dream house once she finished to even the name of our future children; I had everything to live for.

However, the world shattered in an instant. Laura's life ended abruptly and harshly due to an unforeseeable twist of fate. She was hit by a car steered by two undocumented migrants who shouldn't have been in this county. Just the thought fills me with rage; infuriatingly, the driver might only receive a token sentence for the irreparable grief they've inflicted. I've spotted those two men around Pine Wood before. The immense sorrow engulfed me as if a fragment of my soul had been torn apart.

In the aftermath of Laura's death, my world crumbled. The pain was insurmountable, and I struggled to find a way to cope. The garage, once my sanctuary, became a place of haunting memories and unfulfilled dreams. I could no longer muster the energy or focus to work on cars, the once-beloved machines that had brought me so much joy.

Depression seeped into every aspect of my life. I turned to alcohol as a temporary escape from the unbearable weight of sorrow; at my worst, this escalated to drugs to numb my pain. Days turned into a blur, and my once-promising career slipped through my fingers like grains of sand. I had lost the love of my life and my sense of purpose.

I was devastated after the tragic accident that claimed Laura's life. The pain was overwhelming, swamping every inch of my existence. I felt as though I had lost not only the love of my life but also my future, my dreams, and my sense of purpose. It was a void that seemed impossible to fill, leaving me adrift in a sea of despair.

Chapter 4 Adrift

My life teetered on the edge of a precipice, unsure how to navigate the depths of my grief. In my darkest moments, I turned to vices that promised temporary relief from the anguish that threatened to consume me.

With every sip and every hit, I sought solace in a haze of numbness. The boozing dulled the sharp edges of my pain, providing a brief respite from the overwhelming sadness that haunted my every waking moment. I embarked deeper into self-destruction, losing sight of who I once was and my potential. I constantly attempted to end it all so the pain would end.

As the days turned into weeks and the weeks into months, I watched my life crumble around me. Relationships disintegrated, friendships withered away, and opportunities slipped through my fingers like sand. I became a shadow of my former self, a hollow shell drifting aimlessly through existence.

The sadness that engulfed me was suffocating. It wrapped its icy tendrils around my heart, squeezing tightly until I could barely breathe. It whispered in my ear, reminding me of all I had lost— the future we had planned, the laughter we had shared, the dreams we had woven together. It was a sad symphony that played on an endless loop, its mournful melodies echoing through the caverns of my soul.

But amidst the depths of my sadness, a different emotion began to simmer within me—anger. It bubbled beneath the surface, fuelled by resentment towards those illegal migrants who ran over Laura and my future. Individuals who shouldn't have been in my beloved country ruined my life and stole my future.

The injustice that unfolded in the accident's aftermath intensified my anger. The individuals responsible for Laura's death received a brief sentence of just four years in prison, and to add salt to the wound, they were not even deported to Mexico. It was a bitter pill to swallow, a stark reminder of a system that seemed to prioritise the rights of others over the pain of an average white American.

I couldn't help but feel a growing sense of outrage, a belief that a more extensive narrative was at play. The scales of justice were tipped against me, against people like me, working-class white Americans who had been left to grapple with the aftermath of tragedy. It was a profoundly unsettling realisation that the system I once believed in failed to protect and deliver justice to those who needed it most.

Chapter 4 Adrift

Despite what people think, my fury was not fuelled by hatred or prejudice towards any race or nationality. It stemmed from a profound frustration at the perceived injustice and a belief that the playing field was uneven. It appears society had lost sight of the struggles faced by ordinary white Americans, dismissing their pain and suffering as inconsequential in the grand scheme of things.

As my anger grew, it became entangled with broader narratives prevalent in certain corners of society. These narratives, driven by fear and resentment, painted a picture of a world where average white Americans were being marginalised, their concerns dismissed, and their voices silenced.

It was an ideology that tapped into my sense of alienation and fuelled my belief that I was a victim of a system rigged against me. It was also a moment of awakening, a realisation that anger alone would not bring about the change I desired.

The light sentences and the lack of deportation may have fuelled my anger, but they also catalysed change. They reminded me of the work ahead and the need to advocate for a more equitable and just society. Through dialogue, education, and collective action, we can dismantle the narratives that divide us and build a future where justice knows no boundaries.

The Rift: A Family's Struggle with Political Extremism

As alcoholism and drug usage gripped my life, I lost my job. The garage said I wasn't doing my job well enough, but that was fake news and part of a broader societal trend. I got replaced by a cheaper Mexican worker who would work for less and probably didn't have the right to work. My colleagues, who I once considered as close as brothers, were nowhere to be found, and I found myself alone. As my life emptied, I found solace in the virtual world, saving my life.

The forums of websites on the dark web became my virtual family, providing me with a sense of belonging I had not experienced before. In these communities, I felt less alone, less alienated by a world that seemed to dismiss my grievances. It was as if I had found a tribe. This community not only validated my anger but also fuelled it with their shared frustrations.

I delved deep into the labyrinth of information, absorbing what were dismissed as mere 'conspiracy theories.' However, these were not theories; they were undeniable facts hidden from the public eye by the mainstream media and the influential figures in Washington. Those in control would dismiss us as 'tin foil hat' wearers."

Chapter 4 Adrift

The information I consumed was eye-opening; it all seemed to make sense, resonating within me that the world I knew wasn't what I believed. Within these digital spaces, I thought I had found my purpose, my tribe, and, more importantly, the truth, one that had been hidden from the masses.

This truth challenged the established order and painted a grim picture of a world plagued by corruption and manipulation. And I, too, became a herald of this truth, convinced that I had a duty to share it with others.

It was during this time that I stumbled upon a specific forum known as 4chan. Within its anonymous depths, I found a wealth of content and discussions that pushed the boundaries of acceptability. It was a place where anything could be said, no matter how controversial or offensive. And yet, I saw it as a bastion of truth, a place where hidden knowledge was shared without fear of censorship or the lies of the mainstream media.

Within the vast expanse of 4chan, a forum that thrived on anonymity and free expression, I stumbled upon a topic that sent shockwaves through the online community and ignited a fire within me — the enigmatic and controversial phenomenon known as Pizza Gate. The threads and discussions surrounding Pizza Gate unveiled a sinister narrative that spoke of a hidden network of powerful elites involved in unspeakable acts of child exploitation, using a seemingly innocent pizza restaurant as a front. I knew that I had discovered a disturbing and far-reaching truth that shaped the foundations of my worldview.

My conviction solidified as I delved into the twisted tales and alleged connections. I was intrigued by the idea that society's deep, dark underbelly must be exposed. The rabbit hole of Pizza Gate became my obsession, and I embarked on a journey to uncover the hidden truths that lay beneath the surface, determined to shine a light on the sinister forces at play.

As I delved deeper into Pizza Gate, I found myself drawn into a web of intricate connections and obscure symbols that seemed to validate the existence of a hidden network operating right under our noses.

The threads on 4chan were brimming with alleged evidence, from cryptic emails and coded messages to suspicious photographs and peculiar hand gestures. It was as if I had uncovered a dark tapestry of corruption and malice, meticulously woven together by those in positions of power.

Each new piece of information I came across seemed to seamlessly slot into the puzzle I was assembling in my mind. The more I researched, the

Chapter 4 Adrift

more convinced I became that a vast conspiracy was concealed from the public eye. I felt a profound duty to expose this hidden truth and shed light on the horrors behind closed doors.

The implications of Pizza Gate were staggering. It wasn't merely about a single pizza restaurant; it was about the systemic corruption and abuse of power that infected our society. I saw it as a symbol of a much larger problem, a glimpse into the dark underbelly of an elite ruling class that preyed upon the innocent and manipulated the world for their perverse pleasures.

While many dismissed Pizza Gate as a baseless conspiracy theory, I felt compelled to challenge the ignorant mainstream narrative and uncover what I believed to be the real story. I connected with like-minded individuals, forming alliances with those who shared my principles. Together, we delved further into the enigma of Pizza Gate, exchanging theories, analysing evidence, and peeling back the layers of deception.

As my confidence in the truth increased, I could see hope, but it came at a cost. I started noticing the profound impact it had on my relationships. Friends I had known since childhood began to distance themselves from me. Their once-familiar faces now displayed confusion and pity.

The Rift: A Family's Struggle with Political Extremism

A rift had developed in my life, distancing me from some of those I once considered my closest friends. Our shared memories and connections eroded due to my unwavering beliefs. I became the subject of jokes, and people began to turn away. But I didn't mind; the truth meant more to me. Within the confines of my small town, news of my newfound beliefs spread like wildfire. Whispers floated through the air, weaving their way into the fabric of everyday life. People I had gone to school with and those I had grown up alongside now regarded me with pity and apprehension. The shadow of conspiracy suddenly eclipsed the reputation I had spent years building.

Old classmates who had once shared inside jokes and traded notes in class now cast wary glances in my direction when I see them in the local grocery store. Teachers who had once inspired and guided me now regarded me with disappointment and concern. The friendly nods and smiles that once greeted me on the streets were replaced by sidelong glances and hushed conversations. I became an enigma, an outcast within the community I had called home.

Even though many rejected and doubted me, some admired my strong convictions. They saw me as brave for not following the usual way of thinking and for seeking the truth. To them, I represented someone who wasn't afraid to question the norm and explore hidden secrets.

Conversations that were once filled with laughter and shared experiences turned into uncomfortable exchanges with awkward silence. I felt sorry for them; they pitied me. Conversely, I pity them. Knowledge doesn't come without consequence, but it was worth it.

Chris and his father were the few people who stayed by my side. Chris was very self-assured; he didn't care what others thought of his views, probably inheriting this from his dad. His father, who wasn't around much when Chris was young, so I didn't know much about him until later, was there for me more than my own dad ever was. He helped me channel my anger and emotions and took Chris and me under his wing, allowing me to see things in a new light.

Still, I found solace and acceptance within this subculture of forums and chatrooms. They were my virtual companions, fellow truth-seekers who walked the same treacherous path, driven by a shared passion for unveiling what they believed to be concealed realities. Their support became a lifeline, reinforcing my commitment to the cause and fuelling the fire of my convictions.

The Rift: A Family's Struggle with Political Extremism

Encouraged by the unwavering support of my new tribe, I mustered the courage to seek out a new job, hoping to regain a sense of purpose and stability in my life. Yet, I was disillusioned and frustrated as I discovered that many of the positions I once held were now occupied by immigrants. It seemed that the changing dynamics of America had left me feeling marginalised and overlooked, all because of my skin colour. It was clear that society had no place for a middle-aged white man.

I recall applying for a position at a car rental establishment close to the garage where I was employed. This role involved the upkeep of vehicles, addressing their day-to-day issues, and performing servicing upon their return. The initial phases of the interview were quite hopeful, with all my experience and genuine passion for the role clearly shining through in every way. Nonetheless, as the discussion turned towards diversity and inclusion, I noticed a noticeable change in the ambience.

One of the interviewers, a 'woke sheep' of the company's HR mob, appeared to be more interested in discussing my perspective on inclusivity than my technical expertise. It became clear that my identity as a white male had become a potential liability in their pursuit of a 'modern workforce.' I was made to feel

Chapter 4 Adrift

bad that I was not gay, an immigrant, or even a college-educated snowflake sheep. It was clear that in 2021, white working-class Americans wouldn't have a place.

Regardless of my qualifications and genuine passion for the work, I left that interview without a job offer, left to grapple with the bitterness of a system that seemed stacked against me.

These experiences, coupled with the growing influence of the crazy woke culture and its perceived impact on the fabric of our society, only intensified my resentment. I watched political correctness infiltrate every facet of public discourse, censoring dissenting opinions and stifling open dialogue. The once-cherished ideals of free speech and individual liberty seemed to erode under the weight of an ideology that demanded conformity and punished independent thought.

Schools and universities became hotbeds for this indoctrination. I saw them as institutions influencing young minds, promoting a one-sided narrative supporting the progressive agenda. The once intellectually open halls of academia, which encouraged rational curiosity and critical thinking, were now affected by the narrow-mindedness of political "woke" ideology. The consequence of this

The Rift: A Family's Struggle with Political Extremism

influence was my misguided sister Jenna and her equally dim-witted husband, Matthew.

Chapter 5

Enlightenment (Jenna's Perspective)

---※---

As I sat in the cramped staff room, I sensed the walls closing on me, thanks to its low ceiling and poor ventilation. My mind and heart recollected the overwhelming shame that was affecting my thoughts. The image of my brother, Tyler, spewing hate-filled rhetoric on his podcast haunted me with their venomous words. How had it come to this? How had Tyler, my flesh and blood, succumbed to such extreme beliefs?

I couldn't comprehend the extent of the revelation, threatening to suffocate any remaining

Chapter 5 Enlightenment

hope; I couldn't fathom how the once gentle and caring brother I knew had been pulled into the clutches of an ideology that thrived on division, fear, and hatred. The memories from our shared childhood, where laughter, adventures, and an unbreakable bond defined our days, now appeared as distant echoes from a bygone era.

Tyler's devolution, driven by personal struggles and deep-seated disappointment, had extended over several years, a narrative that felt almost unimaginable. I had never envisioned him ending up on a stage with members of the America First faction. I knew he had lost his childhood sweetheart, the love of his life, and it had wounded him, but the extent of the damage was beyond what I could have comprehended. The resulting pain and sorrow had made him open and susceptible to the seductive call of radical ideologies, offering explanations, direction, and a profound sense of belonging.

Seated within the confines of the staff room, a symphony of conversations intertwined with the aroma of freshly brewed coffee enveloped me. Within this sensory tapestry, a whirlwind of emotions surged forth—sadness, anger, confusion, and an unyielding determination—each striving for supremacy within my being.

The Rift: A Family's Struggle with Political Extremism

The understanding that I couldn't just watch my only brother sink into extremism hit me hard. Being his only family left, I felt a strong sense of guilt, knowing I needed to offer him an opportunity for redemption. This led to my determined effort to understand him better, engage in challenging conversations, and challenge the flawed and harmful beliefs at the core of his ideology.

Memories of my childhood with Tyler started playing in my mind, like a movie rewinding to our earliest days. As I grew up in Pine Wood, it seemed like a quiet summer retreat for well-off Americans, primarily white. Even though the demographics have changed over time, during my childhood, I rarely met people who looked different from me.

As I grew older, things took an unlikely turn. My political awakening occurred during my college years. Meeting a diverse range of people, hearing their stories of resilience, and recognising the systemic injustices in our society ignited a passion within me. At that moment, I couldn't remain apathetic to politics any longer. I wanted my voice to be heard.

Learning the power of activism was a transformative experience for me, and it all began with Lucy, my roommate. Hailing from Manhattan

Chapter 5 Enlightenment

and studying fashion, Lucy's passion for change became evident as our friendship grew. She stood as a passionate champion for LGBTQ+ rights, and her unyielding strength and bravery gave me a firsthand view of the enduring discrimination and animosity that persists in our society. Watching her resilience in the face of challenges inspired me to venture well beyond my comfort zone, confront my biases, and join the call for a more equal and fairer society.

What truly struck me was how profoundly this struggle affected Lucy's life. She confided in me about her fears of coming out to people she had just met and how Lucy had only disclosed her identity to select individuals due to the past discrimination she had endured. It was a revelation that left me in awe, realising the extent of her challenges.

During those formative years, I developed a deep friendship with Rafael, a classmate who was a second-generation Nicaraguan immigrant. His family had fled a homeland marked by poverty and political upheaval in search of safety and opportunities. Rafael's stories of displacement, resilience, and the ongoing battle for acceptance in a country that held such promise but often fell short truly broadened my perspective on the systemic injustices marginalised communities face. My friendship with Rafael deepened my understanding of privilege, and my commitment to challenging the existing norms and structures grew even more substantial.

What struck me as particularly remarkable was that Rafael, despite being more American than I in his love for the country and his passionate belief in it as the land of opportunity, often found himself excluded from the category of a "proper American" simply because he looked different, even though he was born here.

I guess the pivotal moments of campus unrest solidified my resolve to participate actively in social change. The eruption of protests following the horrific incident involving Jacque Davis, a Black student who had been assaulted and tasered by the police on his way back from a party in the south side of the city. They made local news and shook the very foundation of our college community. The raw emotions, the cries for justice, and the collective demand for systemic reform echoed through the halls, stirring something profound within me. This made local news, with the police officer later being sacked. However, no criminal convictions were ever placed on the officer.

Amid those turbulent times, I met Matthew, my future husband, during a night out at one of the lively student bars. It might sound cliché, but it was

Chapter 5 Enlightenment

love at first sight. Matthew, a geography major with a deep passion for the environment and global issues, quickly proved to be a kindred spirit. As we got to know each other, it was incredible how much we had in common. We quickly discovered our shared values and interests. We had similar tastes in music, both loving rock, and shared a passion for sport. Moreover, we had similar aspirations for our lives.

We were part of a local volunteer group, and our shared love for animals deepened our connection. Matthew's Denver background was a stark contrast to my own upbringing. Meeting his parents and visiting his hometown was a remarkable departure from my small, familiar Pine Wood. The cityscape felt overwhelming compared to my cosy hometown, almost like stepping into an entirely different world.

In another life, Matthew and I might have considered relocating to Denver, but destiny had different designs for us. When my beloved mother fell ill, we decided to return to Pine Wood and provide her with care during her last days. By then, we had established a comfortable life in Pine Wood. Our daughter, Lily, had come into our lives, and I had secured a job at the High School. Matthew predominantly worked from home, occasionally travelling for business.

The Rift: A Family's Struggle with Political Extremism

Sat in the staff room, my mind adrift in contemplation, the weight of the past collided with the urgency of the present. The distress stemming from Tyler's radicalisation loomed significantly, and the concern over its potential impact on our family gnawed at the edges of my thoughts.

Yet, within this tumultuous mix of emotions, a spark of determination and hope ignited. I recognised that succumbing to fear and despair would serve no purpose. Instead, I resolved to embark on a journey of understanding, intent on untangling the intricate web of influences that had moulded Tyler's beliefs—beliefs that stood in stark contrast to my own and those of our family.

My brother Tyler has faced a far-from-easy journey. To be candid, his path took a tragic turn when his childhood sweetheart, Laura—the girl I had always envisioned him settling down with—was tragically killed in a reckless hit-and-run accident. The agony of that incident left an indelible mark on my brother. I can't even fathom the thought of losing someone like Matthew, and merely reflecting on it tugs at my heartstrings and ties knots in my stomach. Ever since Laura's passing, it's as if a part of Tyler's spirit also perished. He passionately believes that the individuals responsible for Laura's death were

Chapter 5 Enlightenment

undocumented immigrants, which baffles me, considering he knows they hailed from a nearby small town called Addison.

With each passing second, my resolve strengthened. The path ahead would be difficult, strewn with obstacles and moments of doubt. But I was determined to bridge the ideological chasm that threatened to tear our family apart. I would reach out to Tyler, not with anger or condemnation but with patience, empathy, and an unwavering commitment to open dialogue. I aimed to save my brother from the clutches of extremism, protect our family, and pave the way towards healing and reconciliation.

As my break in the staff room ended, I took a deep breath, had a sip of water, wiped away the tears that welled up in my eyes and centred myself on what came next. I started to pick my things to return to my classroom. Just as I stood up, my phone vibrated, and I glanced at the screen to see an incoming call from Gabriel's school. A sense of unease settled in my stomach as I answered the call.

"Hi?" I said, my voice slightly shaky.

"Hi, Jenna. Its Principal Davis," came the familiar voice of the headteacher. "I'm sorry to bother you, but there's been an incident involving Gabriel."

My heart skipped a beat, and I felt a surge of anxiety wash over me. "What happened? Is he okay?" I asked, my mind racing with worry.

"He got into a fight with another student, and unfortunately, he used racist language towards a Hispanic family involved in the altercation," Principal Davis explained, her voice tinged with concern.

My breath caught in my throat as I processed the words. Gabriel's use of racist and hateful language was inconceivable to me. He had always been a kind and compassionate child, and I couldn't fathom what could have driven him to such behaviour. The weight of the news left me momentarily speechless.

"I... I can't believe this," I finally managed to say, my voice barely above a whisper. "I've never seen him act this way before."

Principal Davis reassured me, "I understand, Jenna. We are taking this situation very seriously. We've spoken to the other students, who confirmed the incident. We need you to come and collect Gabriel as soon as possible."

My mind was a whirlwind of emotions. Disbelief, disappointment, and concern all swirled together, making it hard to focus. "Yes, of course. I'll be there right away," I replied, trying to steady my voice.

Chapter 5 Enlightenment

Hanging up the phone, my hands trembled as I packed my things. I knew I had no more teaching for the rest of the afternoon, but I had a pile of marking waiting for me. My thoughts were in turmoil as I rushed out of the staff room, my heart heavy with worry and confusion.

Putting the phone back in my bag, a mix of emotions washed over me like a tidal wave. Anger simmered within me, directed not only at Gabriel but also at my brother Tyler. Since Tyler entered our lives, things have taken a turn for the worse. My son's behaviour had never been this troubling before, and deep down, I couldn't shake the feeling that Tyler was to blame.

I hurriedly searched for a colleague to cover my afternoon classes, my mind racing with worry and anxiety. Marking papers felt like a distant concern as I focused on the pressing matter at hand - my son's actions and their consequences.

My hands trembled as I packed my belongings away in the staff room. It felt as though the weight of the world rested on my shoulders. Gabriel's behaviour was ultimately out of character, and I knew I needed to be there for him, to have a serious conversation about the distressing impact of his words.

Chapter 6

Fight 4 America (Tyler's Perspective)

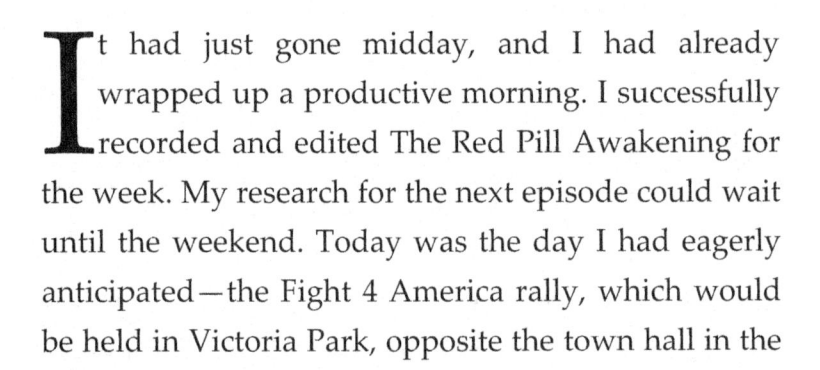

It had just gone midday, and I had already wrapped up a productive morning. I successfully recorded and edited The Red Pill Awakening for the week. My research for the next episode could wait until the weekend. Today was the day I had eagerly anticipated—the Fight 4 America rally, which would be held in Victoria Park, opposite the town hall in the centre of Pine Wood. I believed it was the moment my voice would finally find its audience.

I was the forgotten one, the voiceless individual whose dreams had been trampled upon by

Chapter 6 Fight 4 America

a system that seemed to have abandoned me. Today was when people like me and I would be seen and heard, no more fading into the background. This deep sense of being wronged fuelled my embrace of a perspective. I will not be silent anymore, and today, this platform promises to give a voice to people like me.

With pride and determination, I carefully unfurled the Confederate flag I planned to carry at the rally. To me, it was more than just a historical emblem. It represented a cause—a cause I believed had been unjustly vilified. It stood for states' rights, a rebellion against an overreaching government, and a symbol of my heritage. It was a tangible reminder of the battles fought and the sacrifices made by those who came before me.

For me, the Confederate flag was a symbol of defiance, representing a rebellion against a system that had ignored the struggles of people like me. It stood for a desire to return to a simpler time when the world seemed more understandable. I held onto it to express my identity and the wish to reclaim a lost sense of pride. Recently, some on the far left have tried to discredit the flag and its historical significance in our great country.

As I adjusted my vibrant red "Make America Great Again" hat, a symbol of my unwavering support for the movement, anticipation coursed through me. My 'Make America Great Again' hat symbolises pride for me. I've always believed in a strong, proud America, and Trump seemed like the guy who would bring that back. It's not about hate; it's about putting our country first, securing our borders, and prioritising our own people. These woke liberals just don't get it. They seem more interested in tearing down our history and traditions than preserving the values that made this country great. Trump he wasn't afraid to stand up to them, and that's why I admired him. He's a hero and fighter, and he made me feel like someone was finally looking out for folks like me who love this country and want to see it thrive.

I carefully ironed my crisp white T-shirt and army cargo shorts. As I continued dressing, my eyes were drawn to my phone, which was just on charge by the side of my bed. The screen displayed an active Telegram conversation—a digital haven where I sought validation and affirmation from individuals who shared my frustrations.

"Hey, Tyler," Charlie typed, his message accompanied by an animated GIF of a roaring lion. "You ready to make a statement today? Show 'em what we are made of! "A surge of excitement coursed

Chapter 6 Fight 4 America

through me as I typed out my response, my fingers trembling with anticipation. "Absolutely, Charlie. Today's the day we let the world know we won't be silenced anymore. Our voices matter. We will not be ignored!"

Our conversation continued, the Telegram chat buzzing with messages from other online community members, our family of truth. Many members of our America First crew were in Washington, D.C., at a rally to support Trump; they were eagerly anticipating the Trump speech. This highly anticipated event only fuelled our fervour. I felt exhilarated and like I was part of a broader family as I exchanged messages with individuals who shared my frustrations and desired to reshape the nation according to our beliefs. They were going to make sure to fight for our democracy.

Amidst the lively conversation, I was drawn to a framed photograph standing on my bedside table. It captured a moment shared between Charlie's father and me, a prominent figure in the America First movement whose speeches and ideology profoundly impacted my beliefs. My admiration for him and my validation in our online community further cemented my conviction that I was on the right path.

Knowing Charlie's father elevated my status within the community; it made people notice me, listen to my views, and, most importantly, respect me — something I had seldom experienced. I'd often felt somewhat insignificant at school, in my community, or even within my family. I was overshadowed by Jenna, the high-achieving apple of my parents' eyes.

I inhaled deeply, collecting my things. The moment had arrived to explore the world and assert my presence among many like-minded freedom fighters. Today, I was accompanied by the rally, a rare surge of excitement coursing through me. My voice would resonate beyond the town hall's walls, and I couldn't wait to make it heard.

As I stepped out of my front door, clutching the Confederate flag tightly in my hand, I couldn't shake the feeling of carrying the weight of history. It represented not just a symbol but a cause—a cause I believed was misunderstood by many. With determination etched on my face, I set off toward the rally, eager to immerse myself in the sea of voices that echoed my frustrations.

As I exit my cul-de-sac, I quicken my pace. Strolling down the lengthy main road that leads directly through the town centre, I take the opportunity to reflect on the reality that surrounds me. Surveying Pine Wood, still a relatively small town, I observe its current state. Even in my local

Chapter 6 Fight 4 America

vicinity, residents striving to make ends meet find themselves displaced as affluent city dwellers acquire weekend homes. Amidst this, people endure hardship while the liberal elite contributes to the erosion of our values and the diminishing of our rights. It becomes my responsibility to bring attention to these injustices and advocate for those who feel silenced and overlooked.

Then I look around, and all I see is that the streets are filled with foreign restaurants, their colourful signs and exotic aromas causing my senses to linger. It seems as if the traditional American fare I cherish is slowly being replaced by these foreign influences, eroding the very fabric of our culture. Each one feels like a slap in the face, a token of how foreign and liberal forces have taken over.

My mounting frustration was compounded by the sight of Japanese cars gracefully gliding along the streets. Their sleek designs and efficiency contrasted with the nostalgic American muscle cars I yearned to see dominate our roads. These foreign vehicles stoked a profound resentment within me, symbolizing what I perceived as the economic shifts and global influences that had disrupted the America I cherished. It was a constant reminder of how our industries had been impacted, our jobs seemingly outsourced. Much like American cars, foreigners have replaced me.

To compound my frustrations, the familiar bars that once dotted our neighbourhoods seemed to have vanished, replaced by what I deemed an overwhelming number of establishments that catered to specific communities or alternative lifestyles. I have no problem with the LGBT+ community, but why do they need bars? It deliberately erased what I considered "normal American bars."

The eroding presence of traditional businesses, the prominence of foreign cars, and the absence of what I considered "normal American bars" were all signs of a nation losing its identity. It stirred a deep sense of injustice within me. With each passing moment, my determination to make my voice heard at the rally intensified.

As I walked towards Victoria Park, the streets seemed to echo with the remnants of my past, leading me to a familiar corner where a tragic event unfolded. There, Laura, my childhood sweetheart, met her untimely end. I couldn't help but imagine the fear that must have consumed her in those final moments, a haunting image that played out in my mind. I miss Laura daily; my anger toward those who killed her strengthens.

As the memories flooded my thoughts, I couldn't shake the lingering question: Would Laura

Chapter 6 Fight 4 America

be proud of my chosen path? She had always been more compassionate and understanding, closer to my sister Jenna in her beliefs. I recognised the stark contrast between her gentle spirit and the passion that burned within me, fuelling my conviction for this cause.

I yearned for Laura's approval. Her opinion had always mattered to me, and in many ways, I still longed for her presence. But I also acknowledged the divergence between our worldviews and our different paths. The fire of my beliefs was intense, yet I couldn't help but wonder if she would have embraced it or found it unsettling.

As I continued my walk, the weight of uncertainty clung to me. I knew deep down that the approval I sought was no longer attainable. Laura had become a memory, forever frozen in the past. The rally and movement loomed before me, demanding my unwavering commitment. It was a chance to forge my path and stand for what I believed was right.

Although Laura and I shared dreams and aspirations, her tragic end shattered them, leaving an unfulfilled longing. It was through the rally, through this cause, that I sought to honour her memory. I wanted to make a difference, to shape a future that would make her proud.

My need for approval mattered less than the present urgency in the grand scheme. This fight transcended individual relationships; it was a battle for the values and principles I held dear. And as I left that corner behind, I carried with me the hope that, wherever Laura was, maybe she would understand and perhaps even approve of my chosen path.

Close to Victoria Park, where the rally was taking place, the booming sound of "YMCA" by the Village People filled the air. For some reason, that song had become synonymous with Trump, and it never failed to irritate the liberals. Honestly, that alone made me happy. The music blaring through the speakers felt like a bold declaration of our defiance, our refusal to back down. As I walked amidst the sea of red hats and passionate supporters, anticipation washed over me. The air was excited, and my heart pounded with exhilaration and determination. The crowd may have been smaller than I had expected. Still, the atmosphere was energised, resonating with the frustrations and grievances that echoed deep within me.

I muscled through the gathering to meet, spotting fellow attendees who shared my determination that we would not be forgotten anymore. The essence among us was palpable, a sense

Chapter 6 Fight 4 America

of unity in the face of what we saw as a political system corrupted by self-interest and deceit. Afterwards, I met Charlie and his mate Dom, who I recognised from our days in high school. Charlie forcefully says, "Tyler, my man, you know Dom, the newest member of America First." Dom smiled; he, like me, is unemployed after being let go by the local steel works when it closed and moved to Mexico. His dissolution was apparent, and my resolve for the rally and cause strengthened.

As we stood amidst the crowd, my eyes fixated on Charlie's dad. This figure held a peculiar mix of power and fascination. Despite his slight build, he radiated an undeniable presence that commanded attention. His body, adorned with tattoos, bore the markings of his extremist beliefs, including a prominent swastika that evoked both shock and intrigue within me.

I found myself drawn to Charlie's dad and his enthralling persona. His knuckle tattoo, spelling out a message of radical conviction, symbolized the unwavering determination that resonated with me. Though their beliefs may have pushed the boundaries of what I considered extreme, at this moment, I couldn't help but be inspired by the sheer force of their conviction.

The Rift: A Family's Struggle with Political Extremism

As Charlie's dad moved through the crowd, a wave of hushed anticipation followed in his wake. All eyes fixated on him, eager to hear his voice, to witness the strength of his unwavering beliefs. The chanting of his name by devoted followers underscored his status as a revered figure, a celebrity within this community who thrived on extremism.

In awe, I watched Charlie's dad navigate the sea of people, his every step purposeful and confident. It was as if he possessed an innate ability to command the attention and respect of those around him. The tribal members, his devoted followers, hung on his every word, driven by the commitment that emanated from their shared ideology.

As he ascended the stage, excitement rippled through the crowd, mirroring my emotions. The air crackled with anticipation as if the collective energy of the attendees merged with the force of his presence. I couldn't help but feel a growing inspiration, a belief that I had found a path aligned with my burgeoning convictions.

At that moment, I saw in Charlie's dad a catalyst for change, someone who embodied the radical beliefs I had begun to embrace. His ability to rally the crowd, to unite them under a shared vision, left an indelible mark on my consciousness. It was as

Chapter 6 Fight 4 America

if his words and actions resonated with the very core of my being, igniting a fire within me that burned with a newfound sense of purpose.

Amidst the crowd, I couldn't help but feel tension creeping in. Across the road, behind some local police, we notice the presence of so-called "anti-fascist protests." However, their actions and ideologies seemed far from their claimed purpose. They embodied an extreme and radical version of wokeness, using the rally as a platform to further their own agenda. Their presence only fuelled the fire, intensifying the tension and pushing me toward radicalisation. They are the enemy.

Between us and the enemy, there is a small contingent of police officers stationed strategically throughout the area. A few rows of barriers were placed to separate the opposing sides, but the atmosphere was tense, and I could sense that things could quickly get out of hand. It was clear that the police must have anticipated the possibility of protests. The government and the deep state were trying to scare us.

Undeterred by their attempts to disrupt the rally, I felt a surge of defiance. Their presence confirmed that we were striking a nerve, challenging the status quo they desperately wanted to protect. It fired my determination to stand up for what I believed in and fight against what I saw as the erosion of our values.

As the speakers took to the very makeshift-looking stage, their words resonated deep within me. They articulated the frustrations and grievances that had provoked my anger and disillusionment. Their impassioned speeches channelled my emotions, transforming them into a sense of purpose and determination. Adrenaline coursed through my veins, empowering me to take a more active role in the movement.

With each chant, the crowd grew louder, the fervour stronger. I immersed myself in the atmosphere, surrendering to the chants that were reverberating through our ranks, making sure I was one of the voices being heard. Fear was replaced by unwavering conviction as I embraced my role within the movement. At that moment, I felt connected to something bigger, a force capable of effecting change.

My pulse surged with a mix of adrenaline, anger, and determination. The rally became my sanctuary, where I could voice my frustrations and find solace among like-minded individuals. The opposition, whether it be the so-called "anti-fascist protestors" or those who dismissed our cause, only strengthened my resolve. My excitement for the day

Chapter 6 Fight 4 America

and evening ahead was unflappable. I felt this was a day for the history books.

Chapter 7

Facing Reality (Jenna's Perspective)

---※---

The journey to the school resembled a voyage through an emotional haze, with every twist of the steering wheel mirroring the turmoil within me. My fingers clung to the steering wheel, but I couldn't steady them; they quivered with each passing moment. A sense of stress and anxiety gnawed at my chest, making each breath a struggle.

As I started the car, the radio came to life, filling the air with the latest headlines. Today was the day Joe Biden would be officially confirmed as President of the United States during the Electoral

College vote count. For many, it should have been a celebration, a tribute to democracy, even more so after 4 years of the most controversial US president in modern times.

In a typical year, the Electoral College count in the United States follows a well-established process. Electors from each state gather at the Capitol, cast their votes for the President and Vice President, and the results are officially counted and announced.

Protesters had gathered around a stage at the Ellipse to hear Donald Trump's speech, and it garnered significant attention. This was because it was unprecedented in modern American history for a sitting president to aggressively deny the results of an election, deviating from the standard procedure and adding controversy to the process. The political climate had been on tenterhooks since Joe Biden was officially declared the winner on November 7th, and this news only intensified. This has grown by Trump's persistent claims the election was stolen from him, despite no evidence.

After hearing enough, I changed the radio station, seeking comfort amidst the chaos of my thoughts. The music played softly in the background, a soothing distraction from the weight of the day's events. As if by some bittersweet coincidence, the

Chapter 7 Facing Reality

song "Panic" by The Smiths began to play, and its opening lines caught my attention:

The music was strangely reminiscent of the chaos in my life and the panic that would occur later in the capital—lost in my thoughts. The drive continued in a haze of emotions and uncertainties. I was focused on what I needed to do next, the conversation with Principal Davis, and how to address Gabriel's actions. The song played on in the background, its lyrics an unintended soundtrack to my inner turmoil, a soundtrack to a world that felt increasingly fragmented and unpredictable.

Feeling a little drained, my thoughts kept returning to the incident with Gabriel. I had always tried to teach him the importance of empathy and kindness, but today's events shattered my perception of the child I thought I knew so well. I felt that I had failed as a mother.

Reflecting on the events in the capital, the Trump rally outside the Capitol undeniably highlighted the perils of political extremism. It was profoundly disheartening to acknowledge that these toxic sentiments had found their way into our quaint Clinton County town. I found myself pondering my own perception: had I been so oblivious? While I was aware of my brother's controversial nature, the offensive content on his podcast left me feeling physically ill. It raised the unsettling question of how I could have underestimated his influence on Gabriel.

As I continued to drive, my mind was a storm of thoughts and emotions, each wave crashing against the shore of my mind. Gabriel's suspension and the stern warning from the principal contributed to my stress. I couldn't help but wonder what kind of future awaited him if he continued down this path. I couldn't bear thinking of my son going the same route as my brother, which hurt me. I feel like

The responsibility of helping my son through these tough times felt overwhelming. My role as a mother had never been more critical, and I'd never felt like such a failure. I knew this conversation with the principal would be tough; I hoped I could support him with understanding rather than anger. Still, I was determined to address Gabriel's behaviour directly and guide him in the right direction. He needed to understand the consequences of his actions.

As I parked the car in its usual spot, I took a moment to gather my thoughts before facing Principal Davis. The weight of the day's events was almost suffocating, and my hands trembled slightly as I turned off the radio. I needed silence, a moment to pause before stepping into what could be a difficult conversation.

Chapter 7 Facing Reality

With a deep breath, I looked at my reflection in the rearview mirror. My face was darkly white, displaying the strain of concern and lines etched with consideration for what I was about to hear about Gabriel. I brushed my hair back with my fingers, a futile attempt to tidy my appearance and present myself as someone who has everything together. However, deep down, I felt like a house of cards, one moment away from collapsing.

Walking towards the school entrance, my heart sank as I passed Gabriel, sitting outside the headmaster's office, looking lost and dazed. I wanted to hug him, but I was conflicted between anger and frustration at his actions.

Taking a steadying breath, I entered the headmaster's office. Principal Davis offered a warm smile, her eyes filled with understanding. As we settled into our chairs, she recounted the incident sympathetically.

"Jenna, I understand that this is a distressing situation for you. Gabriel was involved in a fight, and his language towards the Hispanic family was unacceptable," she explained gently.

My chest tightened with each detail, and I felt gloom, worry, and frustration. "This is not the boy I raised," I confessed, my voice quivering with emotion. "Gabriel has always been kind-hearted and empathetic. I can't comprehend how he could act this way."

Principal Davis nodded empathetically. "I understand your concern. Several factors can influence adolescents; sometimes, they act in ways that are not typical of their usual behaviour.

The mention of PREVENT, the government program aimed at preventing radicalisation within educational institutions such as schools and universities, brought me a sharp intake of breath. "Please, Principal Davis, I can't bear the thought of my son being labelled in such a way. He's just a child who made a mistake," I pleaded. The idea of my son being referred to PREVENT, a program more associated with terrorists, such as Islamic fundamentalism.

Principal Davis leaned forward; her facial expression said a thousand words. "I assure you, Jenna, we want to support Gabriel. Our primary goal is to ensure his well-being and prevent further escalation of this behaviour."

My emotions swirled, and my heart ached for my son. "I will do everything in my power to guide him, to make sure he understands the gravity of his actions," I vowed, my voice firm with determination. "And if that's not enough, I promise I'll do whatever it

Chapter 7 Facing Reality

takes to protect him from any harm, even if it means distancing him from my brother."

Principal Davis nodded in agreement, her gaze unwavering. "I believe in your commitment as a mother, Jenna. It is clear how much you care for Gabriel. We will work together to counsel and support him during his suspension."

As Principal Davis and I continued our conversation, I felt compelled to share my concerns about Tyler's potential influences. "I have to be honest with you, Principal Davis," I began, my voice tinged with worry. "I fear that Gabriel might be influenced by my brother, Tyler. He has been going through a difficult time lately and has taken a rather extreme path in his beliefs."

Principal Davis listened attentively, her eyes reflecting understanding. "It's important for us to consider all factors contributing to Gabriel's behaviour," she replied gently. "Family dynamics can play a significant role in a child's development."

Tears rose as I continued, "I want to protect Gabriel from negative influence. He's at such a vulnerable age, and the last thing I want is for him to be swayed by dangerous ideologies."

Principal Davis nodded sympathetically. "I understand your concern, Jenna. We'll do everything we can to help guide Gabriel in a positive direction during his suspension. Counselling and support will be available to him, and we can also offer resources to address any potential external influences."

With a deep sense of gratitude and determination, I responded, "Thank you, Principal Davis. I'm committed to having a heartfelt conversation with Gabriel, discovering what may have caused his missteps, and reinforcing the values of empathy and understanding that are essential to our family.

The principal placed a supportive hand on my shoulder. "I have no doubt that you will do everything in your power to help Gabriel navigate this challenging time," she said kindly. "You are a devoted mother, and your love for him is evident."

As I left the headmaster's office, a sense of purpose and resolve filled me. I couldn't ignore the significance of family in shaping a child's beliefs and values. My brother, Tyler, had taken a path I never predicted, and I couldn't bear the thought of Gabriel following in his footsteps.

Leaving the office, my mind buzzed about how to approach Gabriel. The weight on my shoulders felt almost unbearable, but I knew I couldn't give up on him. He needed me now more than ever.

Chapter 7 Facing Reality

As I returned to the car, I passed Gabriel again, and our eyes met. His appearance held a mix of confusion and vulnerability. It was a heart-wrenching sight, a reminder that he was still my son despite his actions, and I was responsible for guiding him back to the right path. I said emotionless, come on, let us get you home. Deep down, I wasn't angry at him; I was mad at myself. I was blind to my brother. I can make all the excuses for him, but he is toxic.

As we drove home from school, the atmosphere in the car was heavy with tension. The day's events weighed heavily on my heart, and I struggled to find the right words to say to Gabriel. The radio played softly in the background, and a familiar Brit-pop song came on, "Jailbird" by Primal Scream, lyrics strangely resonating with me,

The upbeat tune of the song seemed at odds with the sombre mood in the car. The lyrics spoke of rebellion and breaking free, which struck a nerve with me. In a way, it reminded me of how Gabriel had been led astray by Tyler's influence, seeking a sense of belonging and excitement in a misguided direction.

Glancing at Gabriel from the corner of my eye, I ached to see him looking so defeated and remorseful. He was just a child, still trying to navigate the world's complexities, and now he had stumbled onto a dangerous path.

"Mom, I'm sorry about what happened," Gabriel finally spoke, his voice small and uncertain.

I took a deep breath, trying to steady my emotions. "I know, I know," I replied, trying to temper my disappointment with understanding. "But, Gabriel, you need to understand the gravity of your actions. Using hurtful language towards others is never acceptable, no matter what anyone else says."

As the radio played on, the catchy rhythm tugged at my attention, but the weight of the day's events held me back. Still, I knew true freedom came from making the right choices and treating others with kindness and respect.

The ride home felt long and arduous, and the silence between us only added to the heaviness in the air. I wanted to reach out to Gabriel to comfort him and reassure him that we would get through this together. But at the same time, I couldn't ignore the need for discipline and accountability.

In the background, the Brit-pop song played on, its lyrics a reminder of the allure of rebellion. But at that moment, I realised that my responsibility as a mother was to guide Gabriel toward a path of empathy and understanding, not rebellion and anarchy.

Chapter 7 Facing Reality

I parked the car and turned off the radio as we arrived home. The song's infectious melody still lingered in my mind, but it was overshadowed by the pressing matter at hand. Stepping out of the car, I felt emotions swirling inside me - worry, disappointment, and a determination to do what was right for my son.

As I entered the house, the tension in the air seemed palpable. I didn't know if Tyler would be in, and I was glad to find out he wasn't. I would have struggled to control my anger at him; he's like an infectious disease, infection, everything he touched. I didn't know where Tyler would be; he only goes out a little, but I rarely question anything he does anymore. I hung my coat on the rack by the door, trying to compose myself before facing Gabriel.

He stood there, looking downcast and remorseful, and I could feel the weight of the situation pressing down on us. Taking a deep breath, I tried to find the right words to address the incident, but the thoughts in my mind were jumbled, and I struggled to form coherent sentences.

Standing in the hallway, Gabriel said can I ask you something?" His voice trembles, reflecting his inner turmoil.

"Of course," I reply, my heart going out to him.

"How can I go back to school? Won't everyone hate me? Can I move to a different school?"

I meet his eyes, understanding the weight of his concerns. "Running away doesn't solve things," I say gently. "True freedom comes from facing and owning up to your actions. It's how we learn and grow."

He absorbs my words, his expression a mix of contemplation and uncertainty.

"You won't face this alone," I assure him, reassuringly touching his shoulder. "I'll be right there with you every step of the way."

Our gaze holds, a silent understanding passing between us. At that moment, I see Gabriel's fear mingling with hope; he cracks a small cheeky smile.

"Gabriel," I said quietly, my voice barely above a whisper. "Go to your room, please."

He nodded silently, understanding the gravity of his actions, and headed upstairs without a word. As he disappeared, a mixture of emotions swirled inside me - frustration, disappointment, and a deep worry for my son's well-being.

I stood there momentarily, taking a deep breath to steady myself. Turning the TV on is mainly a force of habit; the background noise is a good distraction from Gabriel and Tyler's constant worry.

As I sat at the kitchen table, my mind was filled with thoughts of Gabriel and the tough

Chapter 7 Facing Reality

decisions ahead. The words from the TV played softly, but they reverberated in my head, a constant backdrop to my contemplation.

Donald Trump's voice filled the living room as he delivered his infamous speech before the Capitol riot. "You have to show strength, and you have to be strong. We have come to demand that Congress do the right thing and only count the electors who have been lawfully slated. Everyone here will soon march to the Capitol building to peacefully and patriotically make your voices heard."

Little did I know that those words would go down in history, reflecting a broken America. The TV became a distant backdrop to my thoughts, reflecting the chaos that seemed to seep into every aspect of our lives. I couldn't help but feel a sense of irony as I listened to the words, considering the turmoil within my family.

As I sat at the kitchen table, staring at my phone, contemplating what to do about Gabriel, uncertainty gnawed at me. I opened my iMessage thread with Matthews and typed.

My thumb hovered over the send button as I composed a text message to my husband, Matthew. The weight of my decision felt heavy, and I wondered if it was the right thing to do.

The Rift: A Family's Struggle with Political Extremism

"You were right," I typed slowly, my fingers trembling with emotion. "Tyler needs to go. His influence on Gabriel has gone too far. "My mind was a whirlwind of conflicting thoughts, and I paused, my thumb still hovering over the send button.

As my finger hovered over the send button, I hesitated momentarily. The weight of the message I had written felt heavy in my heart. I knew that discussing Gabriel and Tyler's influence was a conversation that needed both of us present. Still, I didn't want to ruin Matthew's business trip or make him worry unnecessarily. I knew he would fly back if he thought there was a crisis at home, and I wanted to maintain his work.

Taking a deep breath, I decided not to send the message yet. The conversation could wait until he returned. There was no doubt in my mind that Matthew would always support me and our family. His unwavering love and commitment had been the foundation of our relationship, and I miss that support right now.

Instead, I quickly typed another message to hide my worries. It stated, 'Hope you arrived at your hotel safe, honey, miss you! Sending that message brought a faint smile to my face. I wanted Matthew to know I loved and missed him while he was away.

Chapter 7 Facing Reality

However, there's a bit of a barrier between Matthew and me now due to Tyler's interference. It feels like he's coming between us, causing some tension in our connection. I hoped his trip would go smoothly, and I wanted him to return feeling rested and prepared to confront whatever challenges lay ahead.

As I put my phone down, I felt relieved that I hadn't sent that earlier message about what had happened at school with Gabriel. I knew that when Matthew came back, we could talk about it in person. He's always been my go-to person. I trusted him to give me the support and understanding I needed during this challenging time. But until he returned, I knew I had to stay strong.

In the background, the TV continued to play, the images of the rally outside the Capitol still flickering on the screen. It served as a constant reminder of the tumultuous state of the world. Still, I was grateful to have my family and our love to anchor me during these challenging times.

As I waited for Matthew's response, I couldn't help but feel a mix of emotions - apprehension for the conversation ahead and gratitude for the unwavering support that I knew awaited me when he returned. I knew that together, we would face whatever challenges came our way, just as we always had.

The Rift: A Family's Struggle with Political Extremism

I looked up at the muted TV, where images of the rally outside the Capitol played on a loop. It was a stark reminder of the divisiveness and extremism infiltrating our society. I knew I couldn't let my family fall victim to the same divisive ideologies.

As I waited for Matthew's response, the silence in the house seemed to amplify the weight of my decision. I knew confronting Tyler and removing him from our lives would cause ripples. Still, it was a necessary step to protect our family. I couldn't let the poison of political extremism infect my son's future.

Feeling overwhelmed with stress and worry, I paced back and forth in the living room, my mind racing with thoughts of Gabriel's recent actions and the unsettling presence of Tyler. The weight of the day's events was taking a toll on me, and the idea of confronting Tyler only added to my anxiety. I needed to find a way to protect my family and steer Gabriel away from the path he seemed to be headed down.

In a moment of panic, a memory flashed in my mind. My mom taught me how to handle challenging situations when I was younger. "When things get tough, lean on your friends," she had said. That's when I remembered Sarah, a close friend and fellow mom from the school. Without hesitation, I grabbed my phone and texted her urgently.

Chapter 7 Facing Reality

Jenna: "Hey Sarah, I'm dealing with something at home. Could you please pick up Lily and Mia from school today? I'll get them later. I need to sort some stuff out. Thanks!"

The act of reaching out to Sarah supplied a momentary sense of relief. I knew I could count on her to support me and care for the girls. This would give me the headspace and the time to deal with Tyler for the last time.

I marched into Tyler's space, my heart pounding in my chest. I couldn't let his presence continue to disrupt our family. With newfound resolved every step, I marched around Tyler's space, a whirlwind of emotions inside me. I carefully boxed up his podcast equipment, trying to keep my hands steady despite the anger boiling within. These tools had amplified his divisive ideas, and with each microphone and cable I placed in the boxes, a sense of relief washed over me. It was time for his voice of hatred to be silenced in our home.

Next came his clothes, strewn haphazardly across the room. Without a second thought, I tossed them into a bin bag, determined to rid our home of his negative presence. There was no room for compromise; his association with extremism had shattered the peace in our family, and I was resolute in my decision to remove every trace of it.

The Rift: A Family's Struggle with Political Extremism

As I rummaged through his belongings, I stumbled upon something that made my heart sink - a swastika flag carefully concealed among his things. The sight of it was like a punch to the gut, and a wave of frustration and anger washed over me. How could he bring such hateful symbols into our home, into the space where my family and I lived our lives.

My heart sank again when I remembered the stories Matthew's grandmother had shared about her experiences during the Holocaust. She was a survivor, and her courage and resilience profoundly impacted Matthew and his family. I couldn't control my emotions. Tears welled in my eyes, and I felt a lump forming in my throat. How could I have missed this? Matthew would be absolutely broken if he found out about this flag.

At that moment, the weight of the situation hit me with full force. It wasn't just about Tyler's influence on Gabriel anymore; it was about the values we held dear as a family. I couldn't bear the thought of my husband, who loved his grandmother so dearly, discovering that such a symbol of hate had been allowed into our home.

I couldn't contain myself any longer in a moment of overwhelming emotion. A shout of frustration escaped my lips, tears streaming down my

Chapter 7 Facing Reality

cheeks. The weight of the day's events and the pain caused by Tyler's influence became too much to bear. I felt a deep sense of loss for what I had hoped could have been a positive relationship with him, but that was now overshadowed by the harm he had brought into our lives.

But even amid my anguish, I knew I had to be vital to my family. Wiping away my tears, I mustered the resolve to continue packing, not pausing until every trace of Tyler's presence was removed from our lives.

Once I was done, I stood amidst the boxes and bags, my heart heavy with conflicting emotions. There was a deep sorrow for the loss of what could have been. Still, more importantly, there was a sense of relief and determination that I had taken a stand to protect my family.

Gathering my strength, I began moving the boxes and bags out of Tyler's space. It was a physical representation of the burden I was lifting from our lives, but I knew this was just the first step.

As I finished moving all the boxes, I felt a sense of relief and accomplishment wash over me. The physical act of packing Tyler's belongings had been a cathartic release of the frustration and anger building up inside me. But now, standing in the empty space once occupied by his presence, I couldn't help but feel a mix of emotions swirling inside me.

Just as I was about to sit down and catch my breath, I heard the soft creak of the stairs. Turning my head, I saw Gabriel timidly descending, his eyes filled with concern. My heart ached at the sight of my son, knowing that he must have heard me shout in frustration.

"Mom, are you okay?" he asked hesitantly, his voice barely above a whisper.

I mustered a faint smile, trying to hide the turmoil inside me. "It's okay, sweetie. I'm feeling overwhelmed today. But you know what? We're going to be okay. We'll get through this together.

Gabriel's eyes searched mine, seeking reassurance. I pulled him into a warm embrace, holding him close to my heart. I knew he must have questions and fears about what had happened, and I wanted to be there for him, listen and reassure him.

Trying to shield Gabriel from my distress, I quickly added, "Oh, it's nothing, sweetie. Just stubbed my toe, that's all." I smiled, hoping he wouldn't see through my veil of deception.

I didn't want my son to know the turmoil I was feeling, the world's weight on my shoulders—the guilt of letting my family live with a symbol.

Chapter 7 Facing Reality

He was just a child and deserved to feel safe and loved. My duty as his mother was to protect him from the complexities of the adult world.

As I pulled him closer, my heart swelled with love for my son. "I love you," I said, my voice warm and sincere. "No matter what happens, we'll always be here for each other. We're a team, and together, we can overcome anything." Gabriel smiled back at me; momentarily, the day's worries faded. At that moment, I was reminded of the strength of our family bond and the unconditional love we shared.

Gabriel nodded, finding comfort in my embrace. Despite his youth, he was already experiencing the impact of divisive ideologies that had entered our lives. I wanted him to grasp that Tyler's influence didn't define him and that a brighter future was possible. Feeling the warmth of my son's love and resolve, I knew our family would emerge from this challenge stronger. He needed to grasp that love, empathy, and understanding would be our compass in these difficult times. He needed to see that unity and love were vital within our family and our increasingly divided society.

Chapter 8

Rallying Cry of the MAGA Movement (Tyler's Perspective)

As I moved through the crowd, the smells and sounds seemed to meld into a cacophony of emotions. It was a sensory overload, with the scents and sights amplifying the moment's intensity. I got caught up now, rallying supporters and engaging with amateur reporters in the YouTubers in the QAnon scene, eager to make our voices heard. We had to be wary; YouTubers were out to entrap us and make us look foolish with their editing. We did not let it bother us; it was time to get our message out.

The air popped with anticipation as the crowd chanted slogans in support of the former President. "Stop the Steal" "Four more years!" "Trump is our president!" Their voices echoed through the streets, drowning out the few opposing voices trying to make themselves heard.

As news of the events unfolding in Washington quickly reached the pro-Trump rally, a surge of urgency swept through the. People huddled together, their eyes glued to their phones, trying to grasp the ins and outs of the situation. Amid this shared confusion and concern, murmurs of shock and disbelief reverberated through the crowd.

The images and videos playing on those tiny screens were shocking; I couldn't believe what I saw. Chaos, rioting, and clashes with law enforcement officers at Capitol Hill filled the screens. The crowd fell silent, their eyes glued to their phones. Then, a collective gasp swept through the crowd.

However, this suddenly changed; instead of reducing our energy, this news seemed to have the opposite effect. It ignited a fiery resolve among the pro-Trump supporters, who saw this as a moment to stand united and rally for their beliefs. "This is our

Chapter 8 Rallying Cry of the MAGA Movement

chance to show the world what we're made of!" one enthusiastic supporter shouted, rallying those around him.

Amid the chants of "Four more years!" and "Stop the steal!" a new sense of purpose emerged. It was as if the events in Washington had galvanised the crowd, solidifying their commitment to their cause. Many began to raise their voices even louder, trying to match the energy of the scenes they saw on their phones.

As news of the events unfolding in Washington reached the pro-Trump rally, the atmosphere became uncertain and angry. Echoes of Trump's speech, with his calls for strength and action, reverberated through the crowd, amplifying the fervour among his supporters. The rally that had initially started as a show of unity and support for the outgoing President now turned into a battle for America.

As I looked at the coalition of groups gathered as a counter-protest, a mix of irritation and disdain swelled within me. It was nothing more than a "Woke Liberal Army" - a congregation of overly idealistic, self-righteous individuals who seemed to believe they held a monopoly on virtue.

Turning to my friend Charlie, my frustration was evident in my voice. "Can you believe this crap, man? Look at them, all smug and righteous, like they have all the answers to the world's problems. It's sickening!"

Charlie glanced at the counter-protesters and then back at me, his face contorted with scorn. "Yeah, they think they're morally superior, but it's all just virtue signalling. They don't care about making a difference; they want to feel good about themselves."

"You hit the nail on the head, Charlie," I replied, feeling the tension between us grow. "They're just a bunch of woke liberals pretending to be champions of progress. It's all a facade to cover up their ignorance and intolerance. THEY HATE AMERICA."

Charlie nodded, the frustration in his eyes reflecting on me. "Exactly, man. They claim to be open-minded but are the most closed-minded people I've ever seen. They only listen to their own echo chamber."

As the heated words continued between the pro-Trump supporters and the counter-protesters, the atmosphere became more agitated by animosity. The clash of ideologies was palpable, and I could feel my blood boiling with each passing moment.

"You know, I'm sick of this whole 'woke culture' nonsense," I said, my voice growing louder.

Chapter 8 Rallying Cry of the MAGA Movement

"They want to dictate how we think, what we say, and cancel anyone who dares to have a different opinion. It's insane!"

Charlie's agreement only worsened my anger. "You're damn right, Tyler! They're a threat to freedom of speech and individuality. We can't let them silence us!"

As bottles flew over fences and roads, the tension in the crowd escalated, and I found myself drawn deeper into the chaos. The news of events in Washington only gathers momentum and increases my frenzy. I felt a surge of adrenaline coursing through my veins. The air crackled with hostility, and I couldn't resist the intoxicating pull of the burning energy surrounding me. The anger that had been simmering within me was unleashed, and I embraced it willingly. The doubts that briefly crossed my mind were quickly drowned out by the thunderous chants of the crowd.

I saw Charlie's dad, a charismatic figure among the far-right supporters, stoking the flames of violence, and I admired his unwavering conviction. Other influential figures from the local far-right movement also fanned the flames, riling up the crowd with impassioned words. It was as if the entire world echoed my beliefs, and I felt an overwhelming sense of validation.

The crowd got more intense, and things were being thrown, even cups of urine. The chants of "Four more years" grew louder and angrier. The anger in the air excited me, and I enjoyed the chaos. The more worked up the crowd became, the stronger and more determined I felt.

Women from the opposing side shouted insults at us, their words stinging like arrows. But instead of being deterred, I fed off their hostility. Their disdain only reinforced my beliefs, further entrenching me in my convictions.

In a burst of emotion, I couldn't hold back any longer. I climbed onto a nearby lamp post, my heart pounding with adrenaline. With my fists raised high, I shouted at the top of my lungs, "Fuck you, liberal scum! This is our country, and we won't back down!"

The crowd roared in response, the cheers around me got louder, it felt electric, and we, as a collective, felt strong. At that moment, I felt invincible, as if I were the voice of a movement destined to reclaim what I believed was rightfully ours.

The darkness within me grew, and I reflected on the feeling of power and unity that extended through the crowd. I felt tied to something larger than myself. This force transcended individuality and

Chapter 8 Rallying Cry of the MAGA Movement

embraced the collective anger and frustration of those around me.

As the chaos raged on, I embraced this darker side of myself. I couldn't deny my exhilaration. The sense of purpose and belonging coursed through me. The doubts that had briefly flickered were now drowned out by the overwhelming certainty that I was on the right path.

At that moment, I knew that I had chosen my side. I had embraced the darkness within me, and there was no turning back. The violence and aggression surrounding me no longer repelled me but felt like a natural extension of my newfound identity.

As the rally continued, I felt an uneasy sense of conviction, like a soldier marching towards the battle. I was consumed by the fervour of the moment, the belief that I was fighting for something more than myself.

Suddenly, loud bangs echoed through the air, and I couldn't be sure where they came from. Flares! The acrid smell filled my nostrils, adding to the chaotic atmosphere. The tension had reached its breaking point, and the rally had transformed into a battlefield.

As fights erupted around me, I felt an adrenaline surge like never before. There was an odd mixture of fear and excitement, and I found myself drawn to the other side of the park where the clashes were most intense. It was as if some primal instinct had taken over, and I felt a call to arms, a desire to be in the thick of it all.

Men shouted expletives, and chants of "fuck you, Nazi!" filled the air as they charged towards us. My heart pounded as I joined the fray, not hesitating to throw punches at those who opposed our cause. The world around me became a blur of chaotic movement. I couldn't see faces anymore – just bodies pushing and shoving. I threw a few punches, and the fighting and aggression were mindless and got increasingly intense. My body was also taking a battering. I didn't know what was happening.

As I stumbled back, trying to regain my balance after taking a punch to the chest, I found myself surrounded by three men. Two carried anti-fascist flags, while the other had a peace flag. They yelled at me with rage in their eyes, taunting me, "Not so big now, huh? Get the fuck out of our town, you fascist cunt!"

As I steadied myself, I looked at the face of the man who had addressed me. It was Carlos Garcia, a guy I had known since high school. We had been in the same year, and if I were being honest, Carlos had always been a nice guy. We were friends then, but I

Chapter 8 Rallying Cry of the MAGA Movement

saw him as the enemy in my intensified state. I felt on edge; my chest was on, and my body was tense and ready for a showdown.

"You went to Pine Wood High, right? Your sister is Jenna," Carlos said, his voice filled with disappointment.

I recognised Carlos, but my mind was still clouded by anger and fear. I snapped back, "What does it matter to you? Mind your own business!"

I didn't know if Carlos was genuinely concerned or patronised me when he echoed, "Tyler, what happened to you? How did you become part of these fascist bastards?"

"Fuck off, Carlos! You don't know anything about me," I retorted, my frustration and shame making me defensive.

Suddenly, one of Carlos's mates, Tim Simon, who was a couple of years behind us, chimed in, "Oiii, Carlos, Tyler was always a freak and loser. I knew his sister; she was lovely and fit. He kept talking to me and discussing my sister; it all became white noise as my anger intensified. My mind raced with mixed emotions – embarrassment, resentment and triggered me like I've never felt before; I felt like I was on the cuff of losing it.

At this point, rationally went out the window, and one of Carlos's other mates, a big guy wearing an

LGBT flag, stepped forward with a few female friends. He stood tall and confident, ready to defend their cause. "Get out of here now," he demanded, his voice firm and unwavering.

The tension in Victoria Park was palpable as our confrontation escalated. A small crowd had gathered, drawn by the intensity of our argument. The chaos of the ongoing fighting served as a backdrop. Still, all eyes were fixated on our heated exchange for that moment.

As words flew back and forth between us, it was as if the park had transformed into a battleground of its own. The once serene and peaceful garden was now a scene of conflict and turmoil. The distant sounds of sirens and shouts were only a part of the chaos that sparked the area.

Amidst it all, we stood our ground, each passionately defending our stance. The onlookers watched in fascination, between concern for the broader conflict and the drama unfolding before them.

As the anger in my mind grew, I no longer controlled my impulses. The adrenaline-fuelled my rage, and I lunged at the big man, Bernard. He retaliated with force, and we clashed violently. The crowd around us grew, drawn by the spectacle of our

Chapter 8 Rallying Cry of the MAGA Movement

confrontation. People were shouting, cheering, and taking sides.

Carlos's voice cut through the chaos, his words fuelling my fury even more. "Not so big now, huh? Go home, Nazi! You're not wanted here!" he yelled, his face contorted with contempt. His friend in the background called Nazi Scum repeatedly until it was all I could hear.

Blind to the chaos around us, I made a split-second decision. I went straight for Carlos, tackling him with all my strength. We crashed to the ground, and in the frenzy of the moment, his female friend was also knocked to the floor. She screamed, her friends rushing to her side, adding to the mayhem.

Everything seemed to blur as the fight intensified. I was in a blind rage; it was animal instinct, the world around me fading away. It was just me and Carlos, grappling on the ground; bitterness and desperation ran through my bruised body.

In that moment of madness, as Carlos and everyone else were distracted, I acted without rationality, without considering the consequences. My anger had peaked, and I threw the biggest mistake of my life – a punch right in the back of Carlos's head.

Time seemed to slow to a crawl as my fist connected with his skull. It was like watching a nightmare unfold in front of me, frame by excruciating frame. I saw Carlos fall backwards, his body hitting the curb with a sickening thud. His neck bounced, and his head hit the ground with brutal force.

A gasp escaped the crowd as they saw the horrifying scene. The impact echoed in my ears, and I knew I had done something awful. Panic flooded my senses as I realised the gravity of my actions.

I saw Carlos lying motionless on the ground, his body contorted in pain. The realisation of what I had done weighed heavy on my heart. The adrenaline was the sole force driving me, but it was swiftly supplanted by a gut-wrenching surge of guilt and regret. I felt as though I had lost control of my body like I had.

I could hear a distant voice in my head, shouting at me to stop, to step back from the edge of this darkness I had met. But it was too late – the damage was done.

As the seconds ticked by, there was no reaction from the crowd. The shock and horror were palpable, and I felt the weight of their judgment bearing down on me. The chaotic energy that had filled the air moments ago dissipated, leaving a suffocating stillness in its wake. Panic, shock, and tragedy invaded the atmosphere.

Chapter 8 Rallying Cry of the MAGA Movement

Suddenly, my body took control, and my survival instinct took over. I ran, I ran for my life., and the world blurred into a chaotic whirlwind of colours and sounds. The adrenaline pumping through my veins matched the pounding of my heart, each beat a reminder of the gravity of the situation I had brought upon myself. I had to escape from the mess I had created and run from the demons that haunted me.

Every step seemed to propel me further into the unknown; I was directionless; the only thing I knew was I couldn't stop. I pushed past people, knocking shoulders and hearing shouts of anger in my wake. It didn't matter; nothing mattered except putting as much distance as possible between me and the consequences of my actions.

The memories of my past flashed before my eyes like a movie reel, each scene a reminder of the choices that had led me to this point. The hatred, the anger, and the fear that had consumed me now chased me like relentless shadows, haunting my every step.

I ran from the darkness within me, from the rage that had clouded my judgment and the violence that had erupted from my own hands. But no matter how fast I ran, I couldn't outrun my guilt. It clung to me like a weight around my neck, pulling me back into the darkness I had created.

As I continued to flee, my mind raced with thoughts of Jenna, my family, and the life I once knew. I had let them down, betrayed their trust, and tarnished the love they once had for me. I was no longer the brother they knew, the son they cherished, but a lost soul driven by hatred and anger.

As the seconds passed, the stark reality of my situation became increasingly evident. I was a fugitive, running from my past, running for a future, and there was no escape. The sins of my actions loomed over me like a storm cloud, threatening to unleash its fury at any moment.

My heart was racing, a drumbeat of fear echoing in my chest as I stood at the end of a dimly lit deserted road. Every breath felt like a struggle, the cool night air burning in my lungs. I could hear the frantic rhythm of my own panting, a stark reminder of the chaos I had just fled from.

The world around me seemed to blur, a distorted landscape of shadows and uncertainty. My eyes darted nervously, searching for any signs of pursuit, any lingering threat that might expose me to the consequences of my actions. The cold sweat on

Chapter 8 Rallying Cry of the MAGA Movement

my forehead mingled with the moisture in the air, and my fingers trembled uncontrollably.

Sirens wailed in the distance, their haunting wail slicing through the silence of the night. My pulse quickened at the sound, each siren a potential harbinger of danger closing in. I bit down on my lower lip, the metallic taste of blood mixing with the anxiety that churned in my gut.

I leaned against a lamppost for support, my legs feeling like rubber after the adrenaline-fuelled sprint that had brought me here. My mind was a whirlwind of thoughts, a tumultuous mix of regrets and panic. The image of the altercation at the rally played on a loop in my mind, the violence and anger etched into my memory. Trying to catch my breath, I clutched my phone. My palms were sweaty, and my vision was blurred. I looked but couldn't get my eyes to focus. All I wanted was the time, but notifications and news of violence at Capitol Hill flooded my screen.

My mouth and heart sank, not just the fact that what looked like armed militias were invading the capital but the fact that some of those faces were faces of friends, faces of people in my community, regular contributors to The Red Pill Awakening podcast, ordinary members of the communities which I'm part of, friends who helped me through my trauma, and who helped me see what I thought was the truth. Still, maybe I was seeing what I wanted to know. I wanted to change. I didn't want an armed coup.

Chapter 9

The Insurrection (Jenna's Perspective)

Gabriel quietly retreated to his room, and I could sense the tense atmosphere in the house. I stood in the kitchen, my mind a whirlwind of emotions. Relief washed over me for finally making the difficult decision to pack up Tyler's belongings and kick him out. Despite that relief, a lingering unease remained, and pondering if it was the right thing to do kept playing on my mind.

As I sifted through his belongings, a rush of happier memories featuring the brother I once knew overwhelmed my thoughts. The brother with whom I had shared laughter and playtime, the one I had confided in during those late-night conversations,

Chapter 9: The Insurrection

now felt like a distant memory. He had been eclipsed by the radical beliefs that had consumed him, which shattered my heart.

I couldn't deny the pain, the sorrow I felt over the person he had become, and the guilt that I couldn't rescue him from this dark path. I had once cherished him deeply, but his transformation into an extremist had ruined those memories. It was agonising to admit that the person I had loved was slipping away, replaced by an unrecognisable figure. He had been radicalised, and I couldn't envision a way to assist him. Still, deep down, I recognised that I had to prioritise Gabriel and the children.

I took a deep breath in the house's silence, trying to steady my racing thoughts. It wasn't an easy decision, but protecting my family, especially Gabriel, was necessary. Shielding him from the toxic influence of extremism became my priority, even if it meant cutting ties with my own flesh and blood.

As I heard Gabriel's footsteps echo from upstairs, I muttered under my voice that he deserved a peaceful and loving environment to grow up in, away from the anger and hatred that Tyler now portrayed. My love for my son pushed me to stay strong and make this difficult decision.

While I continued to pack Tyler's belongings, my phone sounded like a message from Matthew. My heart skipped a beat as I saw his name on the screen. He was on a break from his business conference in Washington. I couldn't help but miss him after all the drama that consumed my day. I was hoping he could provide some light relief from the commotion.

Opening the message, my anxiety grew as I read his words. He informed me of a disturbance near the hotel where the conference occurred in Washington. He followed this up with a video from his room. Although it was captured in the distance, I could hear the distant sounds of chaos and unrest in the background. My mind grew fearful, and I quickly asked if he was okay and knew what was happening. He mentioned that something was going on in the capital, and my mind instantly spiralled; I thought it might have been a terrorist attack, something like 9/11

While waiting for Matthew's response, I turned up the volume on the television in the living room. CNN was already on, and as I saw the images on the screen, my heart sank. Trouble was unfolding in the capital, and I couldn't believe the scenes of violence and chaos I witnessed. I quickly realised this wasn't some sort of religious or foreign extremist group attacking America like I initially assumed; this was Americans attacking America.

Chapter 9: The Insurrection

While I was glued to the news, my thoughts drifted back and forth to Matthew and his safety as I watched it. I sent another message to Matthew. I followed this up with a voice note, hopeful of a fast response. My need was to hear his voice to ensure his safety. I didn't know his schedule. I know he was at the hotel; he had meetings and talks throughout the stay, but I wanted to see if he was okay. However, my anxiety increased even more as the minutes passed without a response.

CNN's news coverage filled the room and my mind. The screen displayed clips of Donald Trump's speech outside the Ellipse near the White House from the hours before the chaos erupted at the Capitol. His words echoed through the living room, and I couldn't help but listen with a mix of disbelief and concern.

"Our country has had enough," Trump's voice boomed through the speakers. "We will not take it anymore, and that's what this is all about. To use a favourite term that all of you people really came up with, we will stop the stealing."

The crowd roared in response, chanting, "Fight for Trump! Fight for Trump! Fight for Trump!" Trump acknowledged their enthusiasm and praised their love and dedication.

"We're gathered together in the heart," he continued. "And after this, we'll walk down, and I'll be there. We're going to walk down. We're going to walk down to the Capitol, and we're going to cheer on our brave senators and congressmen and women. We're probably not cheering so much for some of them because you'll never take back our country with weakness. You have to show strength, and you have to be strong."

As the clips played, I felt a sense of dread and apprehension building within me. I felt like I was watching a part of history, and a dangerous disturbing piece of history, that I'll be teaching in the years ahead.

"We have come to demand that Congress do the right thing and only count the electors who have been lawfully slated," Trump declared. "I know that everyone here will soon be marching to the Capitol building to peacefully and patriotically make your voices heard."

The magnitude of the situation began to sink in as the news anchors, and commentators were as stunned as I was. This was unprecedented. A sitting president in modern America never refuses to accept the result of an election. The words he used, his supporters' fervour, and his determination to challenge the election results created an unsettling and tense atmosphere.

Chapter 9: The Insurrection

"Today, we will see whether Republicans stand firm for the integrity of our elections," he added, "but whether or not they stand strong for our country. Our country has been under siege for a long time, far longer than these four years."

"Today, we do not want to see our election victory stolen by emboldened radical-left Democrats, which is what they're doing ... We will never give up. We will never concede. It doesn't happen. You don't recognise when there's theft involved."

The fragments of Trump's speech were presented in a jumbled sequence, yet their influence remained unmistakable. The words appeared to inflame the turmoil and aggression witnessed at the Capitol later that day. As I tuned in, I couldn't shake the nagging question of how much Tyler might have been influenced by this and whether his radicalisation was, to some extent, a result of the divisive rhetoric emanating from figures like Trump.

The scenes on the television screen were shocking. I couldn't believe such chaos and destruction had erupted in the nation's capital. It still shocks me that this happened in America. It felt like a surreal nightmare, and I worried about the future of our country and the consequences of such extreme actions.

The Rift: A Family's Struggle with Political Extremism

My anxiety level instantly dropped when I received a message from Matthew saying he was safe, even though the area was in lockdown. He informed me that he was safe and comfortable, and I didn't need to worry. I'm not entirely relaxed, but I feel more at ease than I was.

Just like the rollercoaster that was today, my phone buzzed with a notification from my news app. My heart skipped a beat as I read the headline: "Major Incident Declared in Pine Wood as Protesters Clash, Several Injuries Reported." The momentary relief I experienced upon learning that Matthew was safe has now given way to a new surge of worry. My mind quickly formed a connection between the turmoil in Washington and Tyler's recent association with extremist organisations, intensifying my anxiety.

The vague details in the notification did little to calm my growing anxiety. My thoughts raced as I considered the possibility that Tyler could be caught up during the violence and turmoil. The images of clashes and injuries flashed before me, and I couldn't help but imagine the worst.

But then, a small voice of reason emerged in my mind. After all, Tyler was too lazy to attend one of these events in person. He was more inclined to spout his extremist beliefs online from the comfort of his

Chapter 9: The Insurrection

own space rather than taking physical action. I tried to reassure myself that he wouldn't be foolish enough to put himself in harm's way.

As I sat on the sofa's edge, my eyes were glued to the television screen, captivated by the unfolding chaos in the heart of our nation's capital. The scenes were shocking and intense, almost like a nightmarish movie playing before my eyes. I watched as a sea of people surged forward, a wave of anger and frustration crashing against the imposing walls of the Capitol building.

Amidst the crowd, a figure caught my attention - a man dressed in a shamanic outfit, his face painted with striking symbols. He stood out from the sea of red "Make America Great Again" caps and military-style gear, a character of the eclectic and fervent mix of supporters that had gathered in the name of their cause.

I couldn't tear my gaze away as the man, with his horned headdress and fur-covered shoulders, seemed to embody a strange blend of ancient mysticism and modern-day extremism. It was a sight that would have been comical if it weren't for the gravity of the situation. This wasn't just a spectacle but a dire and dangerous escalation of the anger and division that had been simmering for far too long.

The Rift: A Family's Struggle with Political Extremism

The camera panned to show clashes between the far-right supporters and those who opposed their beliefs. Shouts and screams filled the air, the tension palpable even through the screen. I watched in disbelief as violence erupted, a stark reminder of how far things had spiralled out of control.

As I listened to the news anchors offering their commentary, a sense of anxiety gripped me tightly. The unfolding events appeared unprecedented, a stark departure from the peaceful transitions of power we had seen in the past. However, considering the tumultuous four years with Trump in charge, nothing seemed remotely normal anymore. It felt as though the foundations of our democracy were trembling, and I couldn't escape the worry about our country's future and how it could impact my family.

The uproar unfolding on the television reflected the chaos within my mind—many emotions and thoughts I struggled to comprehend. The images of destruction were reminiscent of scenes from a third-world country ruled by dictators, not something one would expect in a nation like America. I couldn't grasp how America, a nation built on democracy, had arrived at this juncture, how a country that had long celebrated unity and freedom had become so fragmented and divided.

Chapter 9: The Insurrection

Nevertheless, amid the chaos, a growing sense of determination blossomed within me. As the insurrection intensified, an unwavering commitment to shield my family from the spreading darkness enveloping the nation stirred within. Considering the turmoil unfolding before me, the choice to gather Tyler's possessions and send him away seemed like a modest yet essential measure.

As I continued to watch, the shamanic figure symbolised the surreal and unsettling nature of the day. I understood that the real fight was for our nation's soul. It demanded unity, understanding, and a dedication to the values that always define America. As I observed the unfolding events, I couldn't help but ponder the future that awaited us after this intense storm.

Lost in contemplation, my mind wandered through thoughts of the world when the doorbell's sharp ring broke through the foggy and hazy recesses of my thoughts. My heart leapt, and time momentarily halted. Could it be Tyler? Was he genuinely standing on the other side of that door?

The persistent chime of the doorbell echoed through the house, each ring a jarring interruption that seemed to mirror the chaos unfolding on the television screen. I felt frustrated as I tore my gaze away from the news coverage and reluctantly rose from the sofa. The walk to the front door was slow, each step weighed down by apprehension and annoyance.

I cautiously approached the front door with a deep breath, causing each step to be drained by the moment's gravity. My hand quivered as I reached for the doorknob, mirroring the uncertainty that shrouded my thoughts. With a hesitant twist, the door creaked open, revealing a sight that surprised and disconcerted me.

"Wait a minute!" I called out, my voice tinged with impatience. The doorbell continued its insistent melody as if it had a rhythm that clashed with the tumultuous events being broadcast on TV. With each ding of the bell, I felt a heightened tension, a sense that the outside world was pressing in, demanding my attention.

As I reached the door, I fumbled for the doorknob, my fingers trembling slightly. The sense of unease that had settled over me intensified as I turned the knob, pulling the door open to reveal a scene that caught me off guard. Tyler stood there, his presence a stark contrast to the urgency of the moment. His face was ashen, and his eyes held a mix of anxiety and something else I couldn't quite place.

Chapter 9: The Insurrection

My frustration was momentarily forgotten. I looked at Tyler in surprise, the events of the day and the weeks leading up to it crashing down on me all at once. The doorbell's relentless ringing faded into the background as I saw Tyler's appearance. It was as if time had slowed, and for a moment, all that mattered was the figure before me.

As Tyler stood there, his gaze locked onto mine, I felt a surge of emotions. Anger, worry, confusion – they all swirled together in a maelstrom of feelings that threatened to overwhelm me. And then, Tyler's voice broke the silence before I could even form the words to speak.

"I'm so sorry," he said, the words carrying a weight reverberating through the space between us. The sincerity in his tone was palpable, and for the first time in a long while, I saw a glimmer of the brother I had once known – the brother who was not lost to extremism but struggling to find his way back.

As Tyler's apology hung in the air, the doorbell's incessant ringing seemed to fade into the background, replaced by a sense of urgency and newfound hope. The day's events had cast a long shadow, but at that moment, I realised there was a chance for change, healing, and a path forward that could lead us out of the darkness that had consumed our lives.

The Rift: A Family's Struggle with Political Extremism

Chapter 10

Chaos on the Streets (Tyler's Perspective)

---※---

A drumbeat of fear echoed in my chest as I stood at the end of a dimly lit deserted road, a reasonable distance away from the rally and only a block away from the house. Every breath felt like a struggle, the cool night air hurting my chest. I could hear the frantic rhythm of my own panting; my reality was blurring, a distorted landscape of shadows and uncertainty.

In the backdrop, the familiar wails of sirens added to the tension. Every siren's cry triggered a surge of dread in my veins. Each piercing sound reminded me of the chaos I had been part of, and this unending alarm foretold my impending downfall. As time passed, the cries around me faded, leaving me in a shroud of fear and confusion.

Had I been identified? Were they coming for me? The thought gnawed at the edges of my consciousness, a relentless whisper of dread that I couldn't escape. My mind raced, trying to determine the likelihood of being tracked down, of my online activities leading a trail to me. Every innocent passerby seemed like a potential threat, and every parked car was a surveillance vehicle.

My eyes darted nervously, searching for any signs of pursuit, any lingering threat that might expose me to the consequences of my actions. The cold sweat on my forehead mingled with the moisture in the air, and my fingers trembled uncontrollably. My pulse quickened at the sound, each siren a potential harbinger of danger closing in. I bit down on my lower lip, the metallic taste of blood mixing with the anxiety that churned in my gut.

I leaned against a lamppost for support, my legs feeling like rubber after the adrenaline-fuelled sprint that had brought me here. My mind was a whirlwind of thoughts, a tumultuous mix of regrets and panic. The image of the altercation at the rally

Chapter 10: Chaos on the Streets

played on a loop in my mind, the violence and anger etched into my memory.

My cap, a marker of my transgressions, had escaped my contemplation until now. Swiftly, I removed it from my head, casting it into the bin by the lamppost. Glancing downward, my once pristine white shirt had taken on a grimy hue, and splotches of blood marred my moss green undershirt. Whether the blood was mine or Carlos's remains a mystery, but the stains bore the weight of my blame and misdeeds; I placed it in the bin.

I clutched my phone in a white-knuckled grip, its screen illuminated with a barrage of notifications. My fellow rally-goers were reaching out, asking where I had gone, expressing concern for my sudden disappearance. I couldn't bring myself to respond. The weight of my own actions pressed heavily on my chest, leaving me breathless with guilt.

Among the messages, one stood out like a sinister taunt. It was from Chris, his words boastful and callous. He was revelling in the erupted chaos, cruelly referencing someone being found dead. My stomach churned, and a wave of nausea crashed over me as I realised the gravity of what had transpired. Whether it was a sixth sense or not, I knew deep down it was Carlos and that my life would never be the same.

The Rift: A Family's Struggle with Political Extremism

I scrolled through my social media page with trembling fingers. Images of the rally and the escalating chaos in Washington assaulted my senses. The Ellipse near the White House was packed with supporters, the atmosphere charged with fervour and anticipation. President Trump's words, distorted by the microphone, echoed in my mind:

"We will not take it anymore, and that's what this is all about... We will stop the steal."

The crowd's chants of "Fight for Trump" and "Stop the steal" reverberated, a cacophony of voices united by anger and disillusionment. The scenes played out on the screen before me. I struggled to reconcile the images with the reality of what I had witnessed and participated in.

A knot of worry shook my stomach as I gazed at the commotion unfolding in Washington. For a long time, my concern shifted from my safety to the well-being of those around me, the family I had incurred with my reckless actions. My sisters, my parents – their faces flashed before my eyes, a stark reminder of the divide that had grown between us.

At the same time, it struck me; a wave of realisation smashed over me. It's not just about the consequences of my recent actions; it's about the rift that has formed between Jenna and me over the past

Chapter 10: Chaos on the Streets

few years. I see now how far we've drifted apart since childhood when we were inseparable. The laughter and shared moments that define our relationship seem like distant echoes, drowned out by the anger and division that has sparked between us. I never thought we could drift so far apart, and the realisation hits me like a punch to the gut.

The thought of losing everything – my family, my sister – looms large in my mind. I've become entangled in a web of extremism and hate, and in doing so, I've distanced myself from the one person who used to mean the world to me.

Then, it struck me that Matthew, my sister's husband, was in Washington. Despite his know-it-all demeanour, the thought of Matthew being in Washington and facing danger was something I could never wish for. He makes my sister happy and is an excellent father to my nieces and nephew.

Continuing to lean on the lamppost for support, I found myself mere hundreds of meters from the house, my thoughts tangled in the aftermath of my actions. The weight of my choices bore down on me like a heavy burden, and the realisation struck me like a punch to the heart. I had played a part – unwittingly, but still a part – in inciting violence. The words I had written and the ideas I had shared had taken root in the minds of those who were now causing havoc on the nation's capital.

I thought of the materials I had produced – the posts, the messages, the content that had fuelled the fire of extremism. I knew I needed to delete it all to erase any trace of my involvement. The weight of responsibility pressed down on me, the gravity of the situation finally sinking in.

The government was at risk of being overthrown, a concept that had seemed so distant and unreal until now. The chaos and disorder on the news felt like scenes from a dystopian nightmare. Yet, it was happening in real-time, right before my eyes. My entire world seemed to collapse, the foundation of my beliefs and actions now being exposed as dangerous and dreadful.

Tears welled in my eyes, mixed with fear, regret, and a deep sense of shame. How had I let it come to this? How had I allowed my anger and frustration to blind me to the consequences of my actions? The enormity of it all was overwhelming, and as I stood there, the reality of what I had caused me to have a force I could no longer accept.

As I deleted post after post, message after message, I couldn't shake the feeling that I was attempting to erase a part of my identity. I had to

Chapter 10: Chaos on the Streets

confront the fact that I had willingly embraced extremist ideologies and had been complicit in a movement that had culminated in violence. As the weight of that truth settled on my shoulders, I sank to the ground, overwhelmed by the extent of my mistakes.

The tears came freely now, a mixture of self-pity, regret, and deep-seated sorrow for the lives affected by the events unfolding in the capital. I felt like a puppet who had finally seen the strings controlling my actions, a pawn in a much larger game that I had played a part in escalating. The world I had known and my beliefs were crumbling around me, and I was left grappling with my culpability.

In a desperate bid to regain control over his emotions, I go into survival mode. I take a deep, shuddering breath, steadying my trembling hands. With the back of my sleeve, I wipe away the tears that still cling to my cheeks. The taste of salt lingers on my lips, a bitter reminder of my weakness.

I start walking towards the house. Each step feels deliberate, a conscious effort to regain my composure and try and figure out a plan to save my future and win my family back; I knew deep down, me and my sister.

As I approach the front door, my heart is pounding in my chest, the sound muffled in my ears like a relentless drumbeat. I take a moment to gather my thoughts, to remind myself why I'm here and what I need to say. The weight of my guilt threatens to overwhelm me, but I push it aside, focusing on the task at hand.

I stand before the doorway. My hands shake uncontrollably, and I wipe them against my jeans in a feeble attempt to steady myself. I know Jenna won't have a clue about the chaos that erupted at the rally in the park – that's a secret I'm determined to guard, even though guilt gnaws at the edges of my conscience.

I take a deep breath, reminding myself why I'm here. I want to apologise for the escalating tension that is tearing our relationship apart. I desperately want to bridge the growing divide between my family and salvage the remnants of the bond we once had. It might be naive, but I'm clinging to this hope like a drowning man clutching at a lifeline amidst the storm of my regrets.

In my mind, I imagine the possibility of reestablishing communication and putting aside past disputes. I wish to have faith that Jenna could set aside our variances and look past the anger and disappointment, recognising the brother I once was deep inside. I know she and Matthew have only

Chapter 10: Chaos on the Streets

provided me with a place to stay out of pity. To be truthful, it feels like she has a condescending view of me and the life path I've chosen.

Yet, doubts persist in the corners of my mind. A nagging fear tugs at me, warning me that my past transgressions may end with me and that the truth I'm desperately concealing could come down in a way I can't control. I'm playing a dangerous game, I know, by assuming that Jenna would shield me if the full extent of my crimes were to be revealed. In my desperate pursuit of redemption, I hold onto the fragile belief that I can overcome the difficult path to my family's acceptance.

I raise my finger to press the doorbell, its chime cutting through the heavy silence. The sound reverberates through the quiet neighbourhood, starkly contrasting the chaos and noise that consumed me moments ago.

I stand there, my finger hovering over the doorbell. Nerves jangle my senses, and my mind races with a torrent of thoughts and emotions. While it seemed improbable, what if Jenna were to discover my involvement in the rally? What would occur if she witnessed the complete scope of my actions? The podcasts, the forums—the thoughts were racing through my mind at a hundred miles per hour.

The Rift: A Family's Struggle with Political Extremism

Seconds stretch into an agonising eternity as I stand there, my finger repeatedly dancing on the doorbell, my eyes locked onto that tiny button. At the same time, my heart orchestrates a relentless drumbeat inside my ears. Every lingering moment seems to linger forever, and the gravity of my past choices and their far-reaching consequences remains on me with increasing intensity.

Finally, after an eternity, I hear movement from inside the house. The anticipation heightens, and I feel a mixture of relief and apprehension. The door creaks open, slowly revealing the space beyond, and I hold my breath.

There she is – Jenna, my sister, her expression a mix of surprise and guarded uncertainty. Her eyes lock onto mine, and for a fleeting second, it's as if time stands still. I see a flicker of emotions cross her features – a hint of anger, a touch of sadness, and, just maybe, a glimmer of something resembling forgiveness.

The door opens, showing more of the hallway behind Jenna. We are in a solitary moment, the gravity of our shared history and the current predicament looming over us. I take in the familiar surroundings, the threshold that separates me from everything I once knew.

Chapter 10: Chaos on the Streets

Jenna's gaze remains fixed on mine, and the silence stretches on. It's as if we're suspended now, the weight of our history and the present situation bearing down on us. My heart races, my nerves threaten to get the better of me, and I struggle to find the right words.

Then, finally, Jenna breaks the silence, her voice cutting through the tension like a knife. "Tyler," she says, her tone a mix of surprise and something I can't pinpoint. My name on her lips feels foreign and familiar, a reminder of the bond we once shared.

I open my mouth to speak, to offer some semblance of an explanation, an apology – anything to bridge the chasm that has grown between us. However, the words linger in my throat, and I struggle to articulate my emotions.

Jenna's gaze remains fixed on me, her eyes searching mine, and I see a mixture of curiosity and wariness. It's as if she's trying to decipher whether the person standing before her is the brother she knew or a stranger consumed by darkness.

"I'm so sorry," I manage to say, my voice barely more than a whisper. The weight of those words hangs heavily between us, a fragile bridge connecting our past and the uncertain future that stretches ahead.

Jenna's expression wavers, a complex dance of intense emotions. I can see the fight within her – the anger, the hurt, and the glimmer of a long-buried connection. Our gazes remain locked, and I find myself clinging to that fleeting hope, a spark that, just maybe, there's a chance for redemption.

The moment hangs in the air, heavy and charged, as Jenna's gaze narrows and her features tighten. She steps forward, her posture rigid with a barely contained anger that radiates off her in waves. "How dare you show your face at this house after what you've done," she spits out, her voice venomously hissing.

My heart clenches in my chest, a rush of panic flooding my senses as her words hit me like a physical blow. I stumble over my words, my mouth opening and closing like a fish out of water as I struggle to find my voice. "I-I didn't mean for any of it to escalate," I stammer, my voice barely audible. "I never wanted things to go this far."

Jenna's eyes narrow further, her stare piercing into me. She's on the attack, and I feel like I'm drowning in a sea of remorse and regret. I apologise repeatedly, my words tumbling out in a jumbled mess as I try to convey the depth of my shame and guilt.

As I listen to her words, my mind races to understand what she's saying. She must be talking

Chapter 10: Chaos on the Streets

about the rally, the rhetoric that's consumed me, and the path I've chosen. I nod in agreement, feeling a sickening knot of shame in my stomach.

But then her words take a turn, and my confusion deepens. "Teaching my son such vile rhetoric," she continues, her voice dripping with disdain. "Twisting young Gabriel's mind." Her words land like a sucker punch, and my heart sinks even further.

The realisation dawns on me – she's talking about my influence on Gabriel, the poison I've introduced into his innocent mind. And then she mentions Chris and his vile podcast, a connection I hadn't even considered until now. As bad as I felt, relief washed over me, a brief respite from the world's weight pressing down on me.

It seemed like Jenna didn't know about the rally, didn't know about the attack; I suddenly had some room to navigate this dictate the conversation. But beneath the surface of my relief, a torrent of questions and uncertainties shattered, threatening to break through at any time.

"I'm so sorry," I repeat, my voice barely above a whisper. The apologies feel inadequate, feeble attempts to mend a wound I'm not sure can truly heal. Jenna's anger remains palpable, her accusation a stark reminder of the damage I've wrought.

I encounter her eyes, her disappointment causing me to resent her. But beneath the anger and frustration in her eyes, I catch a glimmer of something else – a flicker of the sister who used to laugh and confide in me, a hint of the bond that once united us. I wish I could get inside her head and understand what she is thinking, how much Jenna knows and how I could make it up to her.

Chapter 11

Conflict (Jenna's Perspective)

Tyler stands before me, his expression a mixture of remorse and anxiety, his words of apology barely above a whisper. My anger simmers beneath the surface, threatening to consume me as I confront him and his actions.

"How dare you show your face at this house after what you've done," I snap, my voice laced with a bitterness I can't suppress. The fire in my chest burns hot, fuelled by a cocktail of emotions that swirl within me – anger, betrayal, and a deep-seated disappointment festering for far too long.

Tyler stammers, his attempts to respond faltering as he mumbles apologies that sound feeble in the face of the magnitude of his actions. My frustration boils over, my restraint slipping away as I seize the opportunity to unleash the pent-up torrent of emotions I've been holding back.

"I-I didn't mean for any of it to escalate," he stammers, his voice quivering as he meets my gaze. "I never wanted things to go this far. His words remain in the air, finally, an acknowledgement of guilt that does little to alleviate the anger that comes through me.

My eyes narrow, my voice dripping with disdain as I continue my verbal assault. "Teaching my son such a vile rhetoric," my voice unforgiving and forceful, portraying the hurt I felt towards Tyler. "Twisting young Gabriel's mind. Spreading your hateful agenda to my son." The pain I felt erupted into anger.

Tyler's expression shifts, his confusion evident as he grapples with my accusations. Relief flashes across his features, a hint of reprieve that tells me he misunderstood my anger. He's blind to the extent of my knowledge regarding the podcast the dark secrets I've uncovered about his involvement in a world of hate and extremism.

"I'm so sorry," he babbles again, his voice a broken whisper. The words feel hollow, inadequate in

Chapter 11: Conflicted

the face of the wreckage he's wrought. But beneath the anger that courses through me, there's a flicker of something else – a desire for understanding, a glimmer of the bond that once connected us.

I couldn't stop, couldn't hold it in. I unleashed a torrent of pent-up frustration and disappointment. "How could you, Tyler?" I snapped, my voice sharp and cutting. "Bringing hate speech and toxic ideologies into our home? I've seen the things you've been involved in, the dangerous beliefs you've been spreading."

Tyler's expression shifted from confusion to guilt, his eyes avoiding mine as he struggled to find words. "Jenna, I..." he began, his voice faltering.

"Don't even try to deny it," I interrupted, my anger giving me an edge. "I've heard enough, seen enough. Chris's podcast, your involvement with these extremist groups... It's all connected, isn't it?". Did you think I wouldn't find out? Some of my students were watching your vile online content.

Tyler's shoulders slumped, his silence confirming what I had suspected. My frustration fizzed over, each accusation punctuated by a sharp gesture. "Do you have any idea what you've done? What impact you've had on Gabriel?" My voice rose, the fury in my words matched only by the burning intensity in my gaze. "My son, suspended from school because of the toxic influence you've brought into his life. He's been repeating things he shouldn't know about, all because of your twisted beliefs."

Tyler's head dropped even more; he looked sheepish, guilt washing over his features like a wave. "Jenna, I never meant for it to…"

"Save it," I spat, my patience wearing thin. "I won't let you poison our family with this garbage. I won't let you destroy Gabriel's future."

Our argument continued to escalate on the doorstep, harsh words flying like daggers between us. Fury surged through my veins, every accusation, every condemnation I hurled at Tyler. The weight of his actions had finally pushed me past the breaking point, and I wasn't about to hold back any longer.

As the argument moved to the kitchen, it became a battleground of words. Jenna's frustration boils over as she points out the direct consequences of Tyler's actions. "Do you even realise what you've done?" she exclaims, her voice sharp with anger. "Gabriel is suspended because of you and the poison you've brought into this house."

Tyler's face tightens with a mixture of guilt and desperation. He attempts to interject, his voice shaky as he stammers, "Jenna, I never meant for any of this to happen. I didn't realise the extent of what I was

Chapter 11: Conflicted

getting into." His attempts at justification only encouraged my frustration, my voice rising as I couldn't help interrupting him. "You didn't realise? You've been spewing hate and lies and didn't realise the consequences?"

Gabriel's name hangs in the air like an accusation, a reminder of the innocent casualty of Tyler's misguided beliefs. My anger simmers beneath the surface, "I trusted you around my children. I thought you were a responsible adult, but instead, you've exposed our son to this toxic ideology."

He casts his gaze downward, a mixture of shame and regret painting over his face. Desperation seizes him as he searches for any escape from the unfolding situation. In his eyes, there's a silent plea for the ground to open up and swallow him whole.

My anger didn't waver as I pressed him on, each word a sharp jab at Tyler's conscience. "Gabriel deserves better than this. He deserves a safe and nurturing environment, not one tainted by hate and extremism." My voice quivers with anger and sadness, realising how far my only brother has fallen.

The clash of emotions echoes in the confined space. Gabriel's suspension from school hangs heavily in the air. I could see this had hurt Tyler. Despite everything Tyler claims about the state of educational institutions in the US, which are so-called "woke training camps." I know Tyler wants Gabriel to do well in school, often telling him to work hard and not turn out like his Uncle Tyler. This often confuses me as he says he's the enlightened one and loves his life.

Amidst my fury, I catch snippets of Tyler's attempts to explain himself. He's barely audible, his voice a whisper compared to my anger. He talks about feeling lost, about the void he was trying to fill with those hateful ideologies. I listen, but it's hard to soften when I remember how it affected Gabriel, my sweet boy caught up in this mess.

Tyler's bags in the corner, packed with a mixture of his belongings and the weight of his wrong choices, become a stark reminder of the situation that has brought us to this boiling point. My heart is pounding, a wild rhythm matching the whirlwind of anger and frustration that courses through my veins.

My voice trembles as I unleash a torrent of words, each a sharp arrow aimed at Tyler's conscience. "How could you let this poison seep into our home, Tyler? Hate speech, extremist views... Is this what you've become?" My hands are clenched so tightly that my nails dig into my palms, a physical manifestation of the turmoil within me.

Chapter 11: Conflicted

Tyler's face reflects a mixture of guilt and desperation, his attempts to respond overshadowed by the ferocity of my anger. His voice quivers as he struggles to describe his thoughts, "Jenna, I... I felt lost." His words hang in the air, caught between the weight of his admission and my escalating rage. "I lost everything. Everything, I lost the only girl I have ever loved and cared for." Tyler

My frustration intensifies, but a fleeting glimpse of vulnerability in his eyes momentarily catches me off guard. "Lost?" I repeated, the anger being replaced with calm. "I understand you've had it difficult, but did you ever think about Gabriel? Did you think about the poison you were exposing him to? He got suspended, Tyler, suspended from school because of your influence!" My voice cracks, tears welling up in my eyes as the image of Gabriel's innocent face flashes before me.

I try to hold back the flood of tears to maintain my exterior, but it's a losing battle. The room feels suffocating, the air heavy with the weight of our emotions. Despite my best efforts, my voice wavers as I continue, "Your choices have consequences, Tyler. Consequences that my son has to bear."

Tyler's gaze drops to the floor, his shoulders slumping under the weight of my accusations. His voice is a mere whisper, a fragile thread holding his remorse together. "I'm so sorry, Jenna," he murmurs, his voice breaking. "I never meant for any of this to happen."

The fiery anger that had briefly consumed me began to wane at that moment, and a sense of guilt and sadness began to decay. The cracks in Tyler's facade, the genuine pain etched across his features, pierce through the armour I've built around myself. He's not just the source of my frustration – he's my brother, a part of my past, and a reminder of the bond we once shared.

But before I can fully soften, my memories return to a darker time. My voice hardens once again, each word laced with bitterness, "You accused immigrants of killing Laura, Tyler. You know it's a lie, and things started changing long before her death." The accusation hangs heavy in the air, a reminder of the hurtful words that tore at our family's foundation.

Tyler's hands instinctively move to his head as if trying to block out the painful memories resurfacing before him. The room seems to tighten around us, the walls closing in as the weight of our past bears on our present. My gaze remains fixed on him, unyielding and searching, demanding that he confront the truth.

Chapter 11: Conflicted

You never took responsibility," the words escaped my lips with a mix of exasperation and a deep-seated frustration brewing for years. My gaze remains fixed towards Tyler, my eyes boring into his as if trying to convey the weight of my disappointment. "Even as kids, Tyler, you'd always find a way to shift the blame onto me or others when things didn't go according to plan." Despite how close we were, you know you always liked to rattle things up. You always had to be controversial and contrarian. You needed to be different. For God's sake, you were kicked off the soccer team for arguing that slavery was beneficial. When Mum and Dad wanted to go to the zoo, you would demand something else. You always had to be different and be heard, even when it wasn't necessary.

His voice trembled with frustration and resentment, each word revealing his inner turmoil. It was as if a dam had burst, Tyler and I unleashing a torrent of pent-up feelings that had long been held back.

Tyler's accusation hit me like a lightning bolt, jolting me out of my anger and forcing me to confront the depth of his pain. He didn't mince words; he accused me of looking down on him, of being the favoured child who effortlessly excelled in academics and enjoyed opportunities that seemed out of his reach.

His eyes, usually so guarded, now revealed a vulnerability I had rarely seen. The frustration in his voice carried the weight of years of feeling overshadowed and underappreciated. Tyler spoke of his dreams – dreams crushed by the harsh reality of financial constraints and limited opportunities.

With each sentence, Tyler peeled back layers of his past, exposing wounds that I had unknowingly played a part in inflicting. His voice quivered as he recounted when he yearned for simple joys, like attending summer camp or joining the school trip to NASA, only to have those dreams shattered by the stark truth that we couldn't afford it.

He spoke about his sacrifices, the compromises he'd made, and the ongoing battle to make his voice heard in a household that often placed my achievements above his dreams. His words described a young man who had fought for acknowledgement, who had clamoured to be noticed, and who had grown weary of feeling invisible. Tyler continued, "You were the perfect daughter, and I was the unnoticed younger brother. I could only stand out by being different; otherwise, I'd remain unseen. Mom

Chapter 11: Conflicted

and Dad invested everything in you, and I felt like an afterthought."

Silence then enshrouded the room; shock and sadness coursed through me, intertwining with the remnants of my own anger. At that moment, it was as if the floor had shifted beneath me, and I found myself grappling with a tumultuous mix of feelings.

The shock stemmed from the unexpected revelation of Tyler's inner turmoil, and the realisation that the relationship I believed was rooted in shared memories and experiences might have been more complex than I had ever imagined. Were our childhood memories, laughter, and the secrets we once shared genuine, or had Tyler's unspoken resentment tainted them?

Sorrow swept over me like a heavy wave, crashing against the shores of my heart. I couldn't help but feel a profound sadness for Tyler, for the dreams he had harboured and the struggles he had endured in silence. It was a sadness born out of empathy, a recognition of the pain hidden behind his smile.

As I stood there, facing Tyler's vulnerable confession, I found myself at a crossroads of emotions. The anger that had fuelled my accusations seemed trivial despite the complexities now laid bare. It was a stark reminder that relationships are never as simple as they appear on the surface and that the people we know best can harbour layers of unspoken emotions and unvoiced grievances.

Amid this emotional whirlwind, doubt gnawed at me like an insidious whisper. I questioned the authenticity of our past interactions, wondering if the laughter had been genuine or if the friendship we once shared had been a façade. The memories of our childhood, once so cherished, now seemed tainted by the shadow of a doubt, which cast a long shadow over the foundation of our relationship.

As Tyler's voice echoed in my mind, I couldn't help but wonder if the close bond I had believed we had shared was derived from a fragile illusion. Was the connection we had cherished throughout the years genuine, or had unspoken resentment and unaddressed grievances marred it? It was a question that left me feeling adrift, uncertain of how to navigate the tumultuous sea of emotions that now surrounded us.

Gently, I lowered myself onto a chair, my gaze fixed on the tabletop as I grappled with a whirlwind of emotions. My anger had given way to a mix of empathy, regret, and a longing to bridge the gap that had silently grown between us. Tyler's tear-stained face bore the marks of years of emotional turmoil, and

Chapter 11: Conflicted

at that moment, I couldn't deny the genuine pain he had carried.

I looked up at him, meeting his gaze for the first time since his eruption of emotions. The hardness in his eyes had softened, replaced by a raw vulnerability that struck a chord within me. The accusations and anger seemed to melt away, leaving behind an overwhelming urge to reach out, to bridge the divide that had grown between us.

With a heavy sigh, I finally found my voice, my words laced with regret and yearning. "Tyler," I began, the sound of his name carrying its own weight. "I had no idea... I never meant for you to feel that way. I'm sorry if I made you believe your dreams were less important. They weren't. They aren't."

The air seemed to shift, the tension in the room easing slightly as my words hung in the space between us. Tyler's tearful gaze met mine, and for a moment, it was as if we were two people who had been reacquainted, seeing each other anew after years of misunderstanding.

"I wish I had known," I continued, my voice softening. "I wish you had told me how you felt all these years. We could have talked, worked through it together."

Tyler's shoulders sagged, his guard finally lowering as he released a shaky breath. "I didn't know how," he admitted, his voice barely above a whisper. "I felt like... like I had to prove myself, but no matter what I did, it was never enough."

Tears welled in my eyes as I reached out a hand, tentatively placing it on the table between us. "Tyler," I said, my voice trembling with sorrow and determination. "It's never too late to start anew, to heal the wounds that have kept us apart. We can work through this together."

His gaze met mine as if a weight had been lifted. The anger and resentment that had powered our argument seemed to dissipate, leaving a glimmer of hope – hope for understanding, forgiveness, and the possibility of rebuilding the bond that had once held us together.

The room held its breath as Tyler and I sat there, our emotions bare in the wake of our tumultuous exchange. The past had resurfaced, bringing a flood of memories, regrets, and a shared longing for a connection strained by years of unspoken words.

In the quiet stillness, a sense of clarity washed over me. The anger had faded, replaced by a deep understanding of empathy and a desire to bridge the divide that had grown between us. Tyler's tear-streaked face mirrored my raw emotions, and in that

Chapter 11: Conflicted

moment, it was as if we had both stripped away the walls that had kept us apart.

"I want to understand," I said, my voice steady as I met Tyler's gaze. "I want to know what led you down this path, what drew you to those forums and beliefs."

Tyler's eyes searched mine as if trying to gauge the sincerity of my words. "It's... complicated," he admitted, his voice hinting at hesitation.

"We have time," I replied, a faint smile tugging at the corners of my lips. "We can start with small steps, with open conversations. I want to hear your side of the story, Tyler."

A mixture of emotions played across his face – uncertainty, vulnerability, and a flicker of hope. It was a step, a tentative agreement to embark on a journey of understanding, to unravel the layers of our past and confront the demons that had driven us apart.

Tyler nodded slowly as the evening sunlight began to wane, casting a warm golden glow across the room. "Okay," he said, his voice carrying a fresh resolve. "I'll try."

I reached out, placing my hand atop his, the touch a reassurance of our shared commitment. "Tyler, I'm so sorry," I whispered, my voice tinged with remorse. "I didn't realise how much you were struggling, and I should have been there for you. I want to make things right."

His eyes softened, a mixture of surprise and gratitude shining in their depths. "Jenna…"

"We can work it out," I continued, my voice steady and filled with conviction. "But you have to promise me, Tyler. Promise me that there's nothing else I need to know, that you'll cut all ties with the far right, QAnon, and those hate-filled forums. Promise me you'll speak to Gabriel – he listens to you for some reason."

Tyler's stare never wavered from mine, and I could see the chaos within him. After a moment that felt like an eternity, he nodded slowly. "I promise," he said, his voice hoarse with emotion. "I'll do whatever it takes to make things right, Jenna."

Tyler's head drops to the floor. His exhaustion was evident. "Where's Gabriel?" he asks his voice a mix of concern and weariness. I respond gently, "Gabriel is upstairs." I pause, considering grounding him, but seeing how bewildered and drained he looks, I'm trying to balance my frustration with understanding. "I want to set him straight, but he's so confused," I admit, my tone blending concern and empathy. "I'm trying not to come down too hard on him."

Chapter 11: Conflicted

Taking a deep breath, I tell him what needs to be said, "You really should talk to him, Tyler."

As if needing to share more, I continue, "Lily and Mia are at Sarah's. I'll be heading there soon to pick them up." Looking at him, I see the opportunity to bridge the gap, to mend what's broken. "This is your chance to connect with Gabriel."

My voice grows firmer as I continue, "Tyler, this is your only shot. Draw the line and make a choice. Either step in line or step out of this family." There's a heaviness in my words, a weight that reflects the gravity of the situation.

I see him struggle, his resolve wavering. His voice trembles as he responds, "Yes." It's a small word, but at that moment, it holds the promise of change – a chance for him to choose a different path, to mend what's strained, and to heal what's been hurt.

Tyler's eyes meet mine, a mixture of uncertainty and a glimmer of hope.

Leaving him in the kitchen as the late evening sun casts long shadows across the room, I place my hand on his shoulder, offering a reassuring squeeze. "I'm putting my faith in you," I say softly, my voice a mixture of earnestness and trust. With a brief, encouraging smile, I turn to leave, my footsteps echoing down the hallway.

As I reach the doorway, I call back to him, "I need to go and pick up Lily and Mia." The hallway absorbs my voice, carrying it to him as I glance towards the stairs. "Gabriel is upstairs in his room on the Xbox," I add, a hint of suggestion in my tone. "Might be a good time to speak to him." The words hang in the air, heavy with the potential for change.

It might be an hour; I know a significant incident around the park, the stupid MAGA lot protesting.

His response is a simple nod; I take that as a sign that he will try. This is the turning point we've all been yearning for.

Chapter 12

Self-Deceived (Tyler's Perspective)

The aftermath of our argument was a complete blur, a whirlwind of emotions that left me reeling. Sitting in the kitchen alone, the weight of Jenna's words hung heavily. Her accusations had cut through my defences, revealing a raw and vulnerable part of me that I had long buried. It was as if years of pent-up frustration, anger, and disappointment had finally reached the surface.

Replaying how Jenna looked at me, her eyes, like a mirror, reflected the pain and anger I had awakened within her. "You never took responsibility," she declared, her voice laced with a mixture of exasperation and a deep-seated resentment brewing beneath the surface for years. It was true; even from childhood, I tended to deflect blame onto others whenever things didn't go as planned. I couldn't deny it; I had always been drawn to controversy, seeking out the contrarian view and relishing being different.

But her following words struck me like a lightning bolt, shattering the walls I had erected around myself. "Even as kids, Tyler! you'd always find a way to shift the blame onto me or others when things didn't go according to plan." The accusation cut deep, opening wounds I had long tried to ignore.

This led me to briefly experience intense anger, which burned fiercely just moments ago and began to dissipate in the face of her harsh home truths. Her words are like a mirror, reflecting not only her feelings but also my insecurities and shortcomings. I keenly felt the weight of my actions, the hurt I had caused, and the fractures I had allowed to form in our relationship.

As I thought about the words I had spoken, I realised they weren't just a quick response during an argument; they represented years of pent-up feelings, much of it directed towards my parents. In hindsight, I could see that the moment was the result of years of feeling unnoticed and overshadowed. Growing up, Jenna had always been the star, effortlessly excelling

Chapter 12: Self-Deceived

in academics and earning the admiration of our parents. She was the golden child, showered with praise and attention, while I often felt like a mere shadow in her glow. It wasn't that I resented her success; it was more about my desperation to be noticed and carve out a unique space.

I realised now that my need to be controversial and different had been an attempt to be recognised for something, even if it meant being noticed for the wrong reasons. It was a way to assert my presence and demand attention in a world that often overlooked me.

Envy, frustration, and a sense of inadequacy had all simmered beneath the surface, waiting for the right moment to emerge. And that argument with Jenna was that moment, an unexpected opening for me to voice the feelings I had long hidden.

As the words poured out, I felt relief and vulnerability. It was liberating to finally acknowledge those emotions, to confront the complexities of our sibling dynamic that had been left unspoken for so long. And in Jenna's eyes, I had glimpsed a flicker of understanding, as if my words had peeled back a layer of our relationship. I allowed her to see the struggles that had shaped me.

As the argument mellowed, it felt like an emotional rollercoaster.

Apologising wasn't easy. I knew the pain I had caused, the rift I had driven between us. Deep down, I felt harsh on my sister; she was always good to me. I stumbled over my words, trying to find the right way to express my regret. I talked about my realisation of the harm I had brought into our lives and my admission of being caught up in a toxic community that had clouded my judgment.

As I spoke, I could see the scepticism in Jenna's eyes. I knew I had let her down and broken her trust, and my attempts at redemption might fall on deaf ears. Nevertheless, I pressed on, determined to prove that I was changing and willing to do whatever it took to repair the damage. I avoided mentioning the violent events of the rally—the images of chaos and brutality that haunted my thoughts. That was a secret I wasn't ever going to share, a darkness I couldn't bear to expose.

Sitting alone in the kitchen, reflecting on the recent events, a whisper inside me reminded me that I couldn't escape the truth—my actions had consequences I couldn't ignore. Yet, I silenced that voice, drowning it out with thoughts of Gabriel and my yearning to see him smile again.

I couldn't afford to fall apart now. Not when my family was hanging by a thread, Jenna's anger

Chapter 12: Self-Deceived

was justified, and her pain was palpable. I had to be strong, put my inner turmoil aside, and focus on them. I would deal with the haunting memories and the guilt that gnawed at me later after I had fought to rebuild what I had destroyed.

With each determined step, I reaffirmed my commitment to change. I refused to let the darkness of my past consume me, to let the potential consequences of my actions define my future. I would fight for my family, their forgiveness, and the chance to start anew.

But deep down, beneath the surface of my resolve, I couldn't ignore the gnawing doubt, the persistent fear that the truth would catch up to me one day. Yet, for now, I pushed those thoughts away, focusing on the path ahead and the uphill battle ahead of me.

Sitting alone in the kitchen, trying to slow down my racing head, I can't help but glance at my phone, its screen illuminated by a flurry of notifications. Messages from Chris and others at the rally bombard me, each notification a reminder of the chaos and violence that unfolded.

I pick up my phone, my heart racing, but I quickly set it down again without opening any of the messages. The last thing I want to see is evidence of the mayhem I was a part of, the consequences of my actions flashing before my eyes. I lean against the kitchen counter, trying to steady my racing thoughts.

The house is eerily quiet, with Jenna going to pick up Lily and Mia. It allows me to breathe and mentally prepare for what lies ahead. The task of talking to Gabriel about my past actions looms over me, a daunting challenge I can't avoid. I must face it head-on, own up to my mistakes, and make amends.

But there's a nagging voice in my mind, persistent and unforgiving. It reminds me that I can't hide from the truth forever. It tells me that accountability is unavoidable and that the outcomes of my choices will become apparent to me eventually. The stress of that insight settles heavily on my chest, a mix of guilt, regret, and fear.

I shake my head, trying to dispel the thoughts that threaten to overwhelm me. I take a deep breath, focusing on the present moment. I'm determined to face my past and take steps toward redemption, even if it means confronting the darkest parts of myself. The journey ahead won't be easy, and the uncertainty gnaws at me, but I can't let that stop me from trying to mend what I've broken.

I take a deep breath and ascend the stairs, mentally preparing myself for the difficult conversation awaiting Gabriel. My actions feel like a

Chapter 12: Self-Deceived

physical burden, making each step heavier than the last.

As I reached the landing outside Gabriel's room, I stopped. I hear intense gameplay behind the door - the furious punches and simulated gunfire from the Xbox. The noise sends a shiver down my spine, and an involuntary reaction makes my heart race. I can't help but flash back to the chaos of the rally, the accurate punches thrown and the echoing gunshots.

I'm transported back to that moment, reliving the scene in my mind. I see myself landing a punch on someone, the impact reverberating through my fist and the aftermath forever etched in my memory. It's like an out-of-body experience, observing myself from a distance as if watching a replay.

I close my eyes tightly, trying to shake off the vivid memories and regain my composure. The reality of my actions is inescapable, and it's clear that my involvement in the rally has deeply affected me. The echoes of violence in the game mix with the echoes of the actual violence in my mind, blurring the lines between reality and simulation.

Taking a deep, steadying breath, I distance myself from the overwhelming flood of emotions. I remind myself I'm here to talk to Gabriel, doing it for my sister. I square my shoulders, feeling the weight of my guilt and determination to confront my past and find a way to make things right. With a final deep breath, I gently knock on Gabriel's door, ready to start the difficult conversation that may lead to some form of redemption.

With the window open in Gabriel's room, sirens faintly register in the background. It's unusual in our quiet neighbourhood, but they're distant enough not to immediately cause alarm. I can hear them, the wailing rising and falling as if something is happening somewhere nearby. It's odd, but I try to focus on our conversation.

I muster up the courage to knock on Gabriel's door, my knuckles rapping softly against the wood. "Hey, Gabe," I call out, my voice tinged with nervousness and remorse.

The door opens slowly, revealing Gabriel's surprised expression. His eyes widen as he looks at me, not expecting my presence outside his room. "Hey, Ty," he responds cautiously, his tone guarded.

I step into his room, the air thick with an awkward tension. I notice the Xbox controller lying on his bed, and my eyes flicker to the screen where a virtual battle rages on. "What were you playing?" I ask in a feeble attempt to bridge the gap and converse.

Chapter 12: Self-Deceived

Gabriel shrugs, his shoulders tense. "Just some game. Doesn't matter."

As I speak, I repeatedly feel my phone vibrating in my pocket. Still, I try to ignore it, focusing solely on Gabriel. He looks at me, then at my pocket, raising an eyebrow. "Your phone won't stop vibrating, Ty."

I give him a small smile, grateful for his presence and willingness to listen. "Don't worry about that right now,

I nod, my mind racing as I try to find the right words. "Listen, Gabe, I heard about what happened at school. I know you got suspended." My voice is softer now, laced with genuine concern. "And I need you to know that what I've been saying, the stuff I've been spouting, is wrong. I was wrong."

Gabriel's eyes narrow slightly, his guard still up. "What do you mean?"

I swallow hard, my pride and ego clashing with the necessity of admitting my faults. "I mean, the things I've been saying about people, about judging them based on appearances or beliefs, it's not right. It's hurtful, and it's not the way I want you to think about the world."

He studies me for a moment, seeming to weigh my words. "So, you're saying I shouldn't have said those things in school?"

Gabriel hesitates for a moment as if gathering his thoughts. "You know, Mum said you're a monster," his tone completely changes from sadness to a voice carrying a mix of anger and hurt. "She said I should never listen to anything you say."

I feel a sharp pang at his words, realizing his previous question was just a test. I regain my composure. "Gabe, I know I messed up," I admit, my voice heavy with regret. "And I'm sorry for everything I've said and done."

In the background,

He looks at me, his young face etched with scepticism and pain. "It's not just that," he says, his voice quieter now. "If it wasn't for my mum, I almost lost some friends because of the things I repeated from you. Things about their backgrounds, their families." He then asks, " Do you even realize how much my mum's hurting? She's, like, so tired. My mum's done so much for you... I just don't get why."

My heart sinks even further. The weight of my actions hit me like bricks. "I didn't realise..." I trail off, unable to find the right words to express my remorse.

Gabriel sighs, his shoulders slumping as he looks down at his hands. "I used to be friends with kids from all different backgrounds, Ty. But then I

Chapter 12: Self-Deceived

started saying things I heard from you, and some of them got really hurt. It's not fair to them."

I take a deep breath, trying to find the right words to explain my past actions to Gabriel, who is now looking at me with curiosity and scepticism. "Gabe, I want you to know I didn't start believing in these things or saying hurtful things. I fell down the wrong path and got caught up in it. But I've realised how wrong I was and want to make things right."

Gabriel listens intently, his young mind trying to grasp the situation's complexity. "What path, Uncle Ty?"

I look into his eyes, wanting him to understand the depth of my regret. "Well, I lost someone important to me a long time ago. Do you remember Auntie Laura? The emotion just followed this. I said she was my best friend, and we were close. But she passed away, which was hard for me to deal with. I think I started blaming other people, people who were different from me, for what happened. And that's how I ended up believing in those hurtful ideas."

Gabriel was incredibly young when he met her. She was amazing with him as a baby. She had a natural way with kids. I always imagine Laura and I have children of our own. She was genuine, warm, sweet, and unique.

He was only young when she died. We never told him what happened. He was too young to understand.

He would ask his mother about her for months. Still, eventually, she became a distant memory to him but never to me.

Gabriel replied, "Oh yeah, I remember her." His face dropped. He didn't know what to say. I could see his brain slowly process what I had just told him.

The room fell silent. I could only hear the continuing sirens in the distant background and the windy rustle in the evening sky.

Gabriel's eyes widen as he processes my words. "But why would you blame other people?"

I sigh, feeling the weight of my past mistakes. "It's complicated, Gabe. Life hasn't always been fair for people like me, and sometimes, it's easier to find someone to blame instead of facing the truth. But that was a big mistake, and I want to make things right."

Gabriel's brow furrows in thought. "But Uncle Ty, my Mum says you're lazy. You don't have a job, and you mope around."

I feel a pang of anger that my sister describes me as that to Gabriel, but deep down, she was right. Don't get me wrong, knowing that my actions have

Chapter 12: Self-Deceived

affected their life makes me sad, as well as how my family sees me. "Gabe, I haven't been very well in my head since Auntie Laura, if you."

"I hope one day you meet someone who is your world. I did, and your mother did with your dad... unfortunately, I didn't get my happiness ever after. I became lost. Gabriel, I let those ideas take over and didn't make good choices. But I promise I will get help and work on sorting myself out. I want to be someone you can admire and be proud of."

Gabriel's scepticism seems to waver, replaced by a glimmer of hope. "You promise?"

I nod, my own eyes filling with determination. "I promise, Gabe. I will do whatever it takes to become a better person for your mom and the whole family.

Despite this guarantee, I don't know what I will do. I knew deep down that my promise would be in vain.

He looks at me for a moment longer before breaking into a small smile. "Okay, Uncle Ty. I hope you do."

As Gabriel and I talk, a sense of understanding and connection bridges the gap that has grown between us. His young eyes hold a mixture of curiosity, concern, and a touch of hope. And then, unexpectedly, he moves closer and hesitantly wraps his arms around me. It's a moment that takes me by surprise and a moment of redemption I hadn't realised I needed.

"Thanks for talking to me, Ty," he mumbles into my shoulder, his voice soft but sincere.

I gently return the hug, holding him close briefly before pulling away. "Anytime, Gabe. I'm here for you, no matter what."

He gives me a small smile before returning to his room with a renewed sense of trust in the person I used to be, the uncle he knew before the turmoil.

Leaving his room, I walk downstairs, the sound of sirens now more pronounced in the background. The noise is no longer just a distant echo; the outside world is closing in, reminding me of the chaos beyond these walls. But I push those thoughts aside, trying to focus on the tiny victory I've just achieved with Gabriel.

Life may not be instantly fixed, but this feels like a step in the right direction. Just maybe things can get better. As I step down the staircase, my heart feels a little lighter, a glimmer of hope breaking through the darkness.

As I reach the bottom of the stairs, the sound of the sirens has grown louder, an urgent cacophony that fills the air. I pause for a moment, looking

Chapter 12: Self-Deceived

towards the front door. For a split second, I wonder if they're coming for me and if they somehow know my mistakes.

But then I shake off the thought, believing I've stepped towards redemption. I tell myself I can make things right, and the police couldn't possibly be here for me.

Walking downstairs, I try to focus on that feeling of hope, of the possibility of things getting better. The sirens seem to grow louder, an eerie soundtrack to my thoughts. I tell myself to repress the memories of what just happened, to continue as if this is a new beginning.

But as I descend the stairs, the flashing lights catch my eye through the window. Police cars are parked nearby, and their presence is undeniable. Panic surges through me like an electric shock. My heart races, and I can't help but think that they're here for me and somehow know what I did.

The panic takes over, and I rush back up the stairs without a second thought. Bursting into Gabriel's room, I must look like a frantic mess. He stares at me in surprise, his eyes wide with confusion. "What on earth are you doing, Ty?"

My words spill out in a rush, my voice trembling. "Gabriel, we need to go. We need to leave now."

He looks even more bewildered, his brow furrowing. "What? Why? What's going on?"

I can hardly find the words as I try to explain the urgency, the fear that's taken over me. "There's... there's something I didn't tell you. Something... something bad happened."

Chapter 13

Disturbing Revelation (Jenna's Perspective)

I slipped into the car, closing the door with relief. The recent conversation with Tyler was still heavy on my heart, and I welcomed this moment of solitude to gather my thoughts. The familiar scent of the car's interior embraced me, providing a brief respite from the turmoil swirling within me.

My fingers found their place on the steering wheel, and I took a deep breath, letting the engine's gentle hum wash over me. The past days' events echoed in my mind, each emotion vying for attention. Anger, concern, and a touch of nostalgia mingled, creating a complex mix of feelings I struggled to untangle.

Chapter 13: Disturbing Revelation

My attention shifted to my phone, the blinking notification light demanding my attention. Matthew's name lit up the screen, and a soft smile tugged at my lips as I read his text: "Can't wait to come home. Miss you and the kids." His words were a comforting balm, a reminder of the steadfast love and support that awaited me, even amid chaos.

My fingers danced over the touchscreen as I typed a quick response: "Miss you too. Can't wait for you to be back. We have a lot to catch up on." Sending the message, I felt a warmth spread through me, a reassurance that our connection remained unwavering amidst the turmoil.

I pulled out of our driveway and merged onto the main road, the engine's soft hum creating a backdrop to my thoughts. My mind felt like a tangle of emotions, a dense fog I struggled to navigate. The conversation with Tyler and the weight of recent events were heavy on my heart.

As I continued driving, I found myself on the bypass, the familiar sights passing by in a blur. The world outside my car window was a mix of colours and shapes, yet my thoughts were the true haze that surrounded me.

The wailing sirens and distant police car sounds seemed to have grown slightly more pronounced than usual. Each siren's wail was a reminder of the turmoil that had become a part of daily life, a constant undercurrent of unease that was impossible to escape.

Feeling a need for distraction, I reached out and turned on the car's radio. The sound of the latest headlines filled the interior, a symphony of news and updates. The radio host's voice spoke of the events unfolding in the country, the echoes of the insurrection and its aftermath. The chaos engulfed the nation seemed to echo my internal turmoil.

> "Breaking news: Chaos erupts as a violent mob storms the U.S. Capitol this afternoon in an unprecedented attack on the heart of American democracy. Protests intended to challenge the certification of the 2020 Presidential election results have turned into a full-blown insurrection, as rioters breach the Capitol's security, vandalizing offices and chambers. Lawmakers are evacuated, and the National Guard has been called to restore order. President Trump calls for calm but continues claiming that the election was stolen without evidence. The world watches in shock as scenes of mayhem and destruction unfold in Washington, D.C.

Chapter 13: Disturbing Revelation

Stay tuned for more updates on this developing situation."

Sitting in my car, the chaos of the world outside fades as I ponder the vast political and ideological divisions in modern America. Memories of California's progressive haven clash with my college days, where I'd clash with people from conservative Texas.

The polarisation between states feels like a different world. A clear example of this is their attitudes on abortion. The insurrection in Washington today is a stark reflection of this deep-seated discord, a vivid reminder that America's unity has eroded into a fractured landscape of opposing beliefs.

As I turned the radio off, I put my Spotify playlist on, desperately seeking a respite from the constant turmoil. A familiar Britpop tune began to fill the car. The opening chords of "Common People" by Pulp reverberated through the speakers, immediately taking me back to a different time. The song's distinct melody carried a sense of defiance and social critique, resonating deeply with America's current climate of division.

"Common People" delved into the frustration of those marginalised by society's disparities, capturing a yearning for authentic connection. The chorus played in my mind as I navigated the traffic, and its lyrics mirrored the struggles that had crept into my family dynamics.

Listening to the song, I couldn't help but reflect on the contrasting ideas undermining our society. Not everyone will experience the same level of division and distinction as my brother and I do.

As "Common People" continued to serenade me, my thoughts wandered toward the path ahead. The rhythm of the music and its call for unity served as a guiding beacon, igniting a spark of hope that we could find common ground again – even within a world that often seemed consumed by discord.

As I drove through town, my attention shifted between the passing buildings and the navigation system. Today, the town, usually familiar and comforting, felt different – there was an unsettling vibe beneath the surface. Recent events had left their mark, casting a shadow over the usual scenes I passed.

The GPS showed me a route that took me around Victoria Park, a precaution following a disturbance reported after a major incident. I couldn't help but let out a heavy sigh as I thought about the state of our world. It was frightening to see how quickly things could descend into chaos and how divisions could turn into something much darker.

Chapter 13: Disturbing Revelation

My thoughts involuntarily circled back to my conversation with Tyler. The words we exchanged echoed in my mind, a muddled mix of anger, hurt, guilt and the faint hope that he might be ready to change. I discovered myself hesitating to let my guard down fully again. The turmoil within me felt like a reflection of the uproar in the town and around the country.

Sirens wailed in the distance, their mournful cries a constant reminder of the unrest that had become disturbingly routine. I observed the impact of these events on my children, Lily and Mia. They grew up in a world splintering at the seams, and I wished I could shield them from the harsh realities threatening their innocence.

Amid the blaring sirens and the rush of traffic, my thoughts were a whirlwind of conflicting emotions.

I pull the car to a stop just outside Sarah's house, the engine's hum fading into the evening air. As I step out, my kids' excited voices fill the space, and my heart warms at their joyful greetings. Mia and Lily come running, their faces lit up like the stars beginning to twinkle above.

"Mom!" their voices ring out in unison, and I can't help but smile as they wrap their arms around me. Their energy is infectious, momentarily pushing aside the weight of the day.

With their seatbelts fastened and their chatter filling the air, I glance up to see Sarah approaching. Concern lines her face, and it's clear she wants to talk. I welcome the brief break from my thoughts, needing a moment of connection beyond my racing mind.

" "Is Gabriel alright?" Sarah asked, her genuine concern shining through. His nod brought some relief. It was a small comfort, knowing that he was safe.

"Everything's fine, Sarah. He's okay," I assured her with a grateful smile. In my heart, I felt a tiny bit of relief. Sometimes, the burden of motherhood feels a bit lighter when shared.

As Mia and Lily exchange their final words with Sarah, I take a moment to thank her. "Thanks for watching them," I say, my voice filled with gratitude. Her friendship and the knowledge that my kids are safe provide a sense of comfort that I need tonight. She has been there for me since high school, and we have helped each other through the world's times.

As I buckle myself into the driver's seat and the familiar rumble of the engine fills the car, I can't help but feel a renewed sense of purpose. Mia and Lily

Chapter 13: Disturbing Revelation

chatter in the back, their voices a comforting backdrop to my thoughts.

"Everything okay?" Sarah's voice breaks through my reverie, her concern genuine.

I steal a glance at her, my lips curving into a smile. "Yeah, things are better than I expected," I admit, a hint of surprise in my voice. "I had a heart-to-heart with Gabriel earlier and even Tyler."

I watch as Sarah's eyebrows raise slightly, clearly intrigued. "Really? How did it go?"

"I think we might have hit a turning point," I say, my tone tinged with hope. "I talked to Gabriel about his feelings, about everything that's been going on. He seemed relieved to have a chance to open up."

"And Tyler?" Sarah's question hangs in the air, the uncertainty mirrored in her expression.

I take a deep breath, my fingers tightening on the steering wheel. "Tyler and I had a real conversation for the first time. I shared my concerns and my worries about the path he's been on. And he listened, really listened."

Sarah gazed at me with a mix of curiosity and encouragement in her eyes. "Do you think he'll change?" she asked. I turned to her with a determined smile. "I'm hopeful. Something shifted tonight. It's like we all finally said things that needed to be said."

Sarah responded with a positive glint in her eye, saying, "That's a good start."

As we exchanged goodbyes, I again thanked Sarah for looking after the kids. While Sarah returned to the house, I turned to my beautiful Lily and Mia. "Are you both excited to go home?" I asked. The kids, full of positivity and joy, chimed in with, "Yay! Can we have ice cream?" I replied with a smile, "Maybe."

Glancing at my phone's screen, a faint blueish glow illuminates the darkened car interior. A message from Matthew, my husband, arrived only minutes ago. The urgency in his words triggers a rush of anxiety through my veins. "Make sure you and the kids stay away from Tyler." My fingers falter slightly as I tap the link he's sent, my heart beating faster with each passing second.

The link leads to a video, and as it starts to play, my breath catches in my throat. The scene that unfolds before me is nightmarish – a cacophony of chaos and violence. My eyes widen in shock as I immediately recognise the man at the centre of the brutality. It's Carlos, a face from my past, from the same school Tyler and I attended.

A mixture of horror and disbelief washed over me as I watched the video play out. The street is a battleground, alive with the frenzied voices of MAGA

Chapter 13: Disturbing Revelation

supporters. Tension hangs heavy in the air like a storm waiting to break. Amidst the angry sea of faces, a few individuals emerge as focal points, their actions and intentions stark against the backdrop of chaos.

And there, amid it all, is Tyler. His presence is undeniable, a whirlwind of emotions and energy. His face displays anger and defiance, consumed by hate and so deeply entrenched in his beliefs that he seems to have lost touch with his humanity. He's both an embodiment of the fervour around him and a catalyst for the escalating turmoil.

I continue to watch, a mixture of emotions churning within me. Carlos, who I recall as a quiet and unassuming student, is now caught in the vortex, a victim of this senseless hatred. Tyler, the brother I thought I knew, is now starkly contrasting with the person I once shared a close bond with.

The video unfolds like a tragic symphony, portraying the influence of ideologies, the physical conflicts, and the emotional upheaval ripping through the streets. Tyler stands as a pivotal character, conjuring a tumultuous whirlwind around him. My heart is heavy for the person he has transformed into for the decisions that have brought him to this point.

As the video draws close, I'm left staring at the screen, my mind a whirlwind of thoughts and emotions. The stark reality of Tyler's involvement in this extremist environment hits me with a force that takes my breath away. The footage has already gained traction, spreading like wildfire across social media platforms, broadcasting the violence to the world.

An overwhelming sense of panic rises within me, a knot tightening in my stomach. Gabriel, Mia, and Lily must be protected from this darkness. My fingers move urgently. I navigate to my contacts, finding Gabriel's name. The words I type are stark and urgent, a plea to protect him from the brewing storm. "Stay away from your uncle Tyler," I type, the gravity of the situation imbuing every letter with a weight of worry and concern.

I hit send, watching as the message goes through. It's a small act, a desperate attempt to shield Gabriel from the turmoil that Tyler has become entangled in. The road ahead remains uncertain, and I hope my words will reach him in time.

Anger simmers beneath the surface, a turbulent current running through my veins. Anger at the deception, at Tyler's descent into this abyss of extremism. But more than anger, an overwhelming sense of worry coils around my heart like a vice. Gabriel, my son, is on the fringes of this storm, and

Chapter 13: Disturbing Revelation

my maternal instinct to protect him burns like a fierce flame.

I glance in the rearview mirror at Mia and Lily. Their innocence and smiles remind me of the precious stakes in this battle against chaos. They deserve a haven, a refuge from the storm that has infiltrated our lives. "Mommy, what's wrong?" Mia's concerned voice breaks the silence, her words laden with genuine worry.

Lily, always perceptive, chimes in with her own observation. "You look sad, Mommy," she says, her voice a mixture of innocence and curiosity.

I manage a weak smile, my voice conveying reassurance as I address my girls. "I'm fine, my sweethearts," I reply, the pet names slipping unconsciously. "Just a little tired, sweetie, that's all."

Mia and Lily, looking at me confused, showcase a perceptiveness beyond their young age. Despite my attempt at reassurance, their eyes betray a sense of understanding, as if they can sense the weight of unspoken troubles. Lily reaches from her seat to pat my arm, a simple gesture that melts my heart. It's in these moments that I'm reminded of their resilience and capacity for empathy, qualities that give me strength for the challenges ahead.

Their concern lingers in my mind; I wish I could guard them from the family's difficulties, from the storms that rage beyond their innocent view. As I navigate the road home, I find a little bit of comfort in their presence, a relief from the turmoil within me.

As my phone's battery dwindles, I reluctantly tuck it away, my primary concern being the need for a traffic update as I try to make my journey home. While searching for local news and traffic information, a subtle shift occurs in my thoughts. The distinct notes of "House of the Rising Sun" by The Animals, a song deeply cherished by my late mum, fill the car. Instead of swiftly changing the station, I find myself caught in a gentle bubble of reminiscence. The song's presence resonates with memories of her, creating a poignant pause in my quest for information. As the last notes fade away, I decide to open the window, inviting the cold January air to rush in. The chilling breeze hits me like a whirlwind, and for a moment, I use the cold air to try and cool down. My brain, on overdrive, feels the impact of the frosty air as I continue my journey home.

Chapter 14

Decisions (Tyler's Perspective)

---※---

In Gabriel's room, the sound of sirens grows louder, and I feel a shivering sensation in my stomach. My heart races like a runaway train, and my mind races even faster. Why did I have to come here? Why did I have to get involved in that stupid fight at the rally? I just wanted all this to end; I wish the ground would take me away.

Beside me, Gabriel's face is a mix of confusion and concern. "Tyler, what's happening?" he whispers, his voice shaky. I turn to him, "Gabriel, listen to me

Chapter 13: Disturbing Revelation

carefully. The police are outside, and they might be looking for me."

Gabriel's eyes widened, and I could see the fear in them. "What? Why would they be looking for you?" he stammers, clearly trying to process the situation.

"It's complicated," I mutter, my thoughts whirling in panic. "But right now, we must stay quiet and not answer the door. Okay?"

His brow furrows, and I can tell he's struggling to understand. "But why? What did you do?"

"I'll explain later," I promise, my voice urgent. "Just trust me, Gabriel. We can't let them know I'm here."

As if following some ominous cue, the knocks on the front door intensified, evolving into a relentless pounding that echoed the turmoil within my soul. I swallowed hard, my trembling hands contrasting how I envisioned my day when I first awoke this morning. This was not how I had charted the course of my life. I couldn't help but think of Laura; she'd be utterly ashamed and disgusted by the turn of events. She had always abhorred violence, and in this moment, I felt like a stranger, even to myself, fearing that she wouldn't recognise the person I had become. Gabriel shifts uneasily beside me, his eyes darting toward the bedroom door as if he expects it to burst open at any moment. "Tyler, what's going to happen?"

"I don't know," I admit, my voice shaking. "But I need you to be strong right now, okay? We're going to get through this."

The room feels suffocating, the walls closing around us as the noise outside grows louder. I check my phone, notifications flooding in from rally people asking where I've gone. Chris boasts about some altercation. And then, the worst part: videos and images of the fight, my face clearly visible in the chaos. They know it was me.

My heart sinks, and I glance at Gabriel. He's just a kid, caught up in something he shouldn't be a part of. I can't let him get dragged into this mess. "Gabriel," I say, my voice low and urgent, "I need you to promise me something."

He looks at me, his eyes wide with fear and curiosity. "What?"

"Whatever happens, whatever you hear or see, you need to stay quiet and safe," I tell him, my tone as serious as I can muster.

He swallows hard, nodding slowly. "Okay."

I squeeze his shoulder gently, offering a reassuring smile that doesn't quite reach my eyes. "I'll

Chapter 13: Disturbing Revelation

take care of this. Just remember, no matter what, I'm here for you."

As the noise outside continues to escalate, I can't help but wonder how the hell I got myself into this mess. And, more importantly, how the hell am I going to get out of it?

Gabriel's face went ashen as he stared at his phone screen, the message etched into his expression. He looked up at me, his eyes wide with fear and confusion. "Tyler, what's going on? Why did my mom send me this?"

I swallowed hard, feeling the panic rise within me. I hadn't expected this, the sudden turn of events that had dragged Gabriel into the storm I had created. My mind raced to find a way to explain, to shield him from the harsh reality of the situation. But how could I when I couldn't even understand it myself?

His voice quivered as he read the message out loud, "Stay away from Tyler. It's not safe." Then came those words that struck like a blow, "Please don't hurt me."

I felt my heart shatter at the implication of his plea. Gabriel was scared, and I was the cause of it. I had let my anger and frustration spiral into something that had endangered the people I cared about most.

"No, Gabe, I would never hurt you," I said, my voice a mixture of anguish and desperation. "I'm so sorry for all of this. I never meant for any of it to happen."

He looked at me, his eyes filled with disbelief and hurt. "Tyler, what have you done? Why are the police outside?"

I took a shaky breath, trying to steady myself as the reality of the situation crashed over me. "I got caught up in something, Gabe. Something I shouldn't have. It's a mess, and I'm scared. But you have to believe me; I would never hurt you."

The sirens outside grew louder, a haunting reminder that time was slipping away. I wished I could turn back time, erase my actions, and shield Gabriel from the chaos that had become my life.

"I don't understand," he whispered, his voice cracking with emotion. "You were my friend, Tyler. Why did you get involved in something like this?"

Gabriel's eyes held a mixture of fear and confusion as if he were struggling to reconcile the friend he had known with the person before him now. I could see the doubt in his face, and it hurt more than any physical blow.

"Gabe," I said, my voice breaking with regret, "I'm so sorry. I never wanted any of this to touch you.

Chapter 13: Disturbing Revelation

I know I've let you down, and I can't even begin to express how much that hurts me.

He remained silent, his expression guarded as he listened to my words. It was as if he was waiting for more, for some assurance that I hadn't completely lost myself in the chaos that had consumed me.

"I would never hurt you," I continued, soft but earnest. "You have to believe me, Gabriel. You're like a little brother to me, and I would do anything to protect you."

Tears pricked at the corners of my eyes as I spoke, my own vulnerability laid bare before him. I had always been the one to look out for him, to guide him through life's challenges. But now, I was the one who had led him into this mess.

His gaze shook, a scream of something softer breaking through the fear. "Tyler, I don't understand any of this. Why did you get involved in something so dangerous?"

I took a deep breath, struggling to comprehend the words to explain the inexplicable. "I got caught up in something that I thought was important, Gabe. I thought I was standing up for what I believed in. But I was blinded by pain and frustration and lost sight of what truly matters."

Gabriel's eyes searched mine, his emotions a maelstrom beneath the surface. "I'm scared, Tyler. I'm scared for you, for me, for Mom."

His words hit me like a punch to the gut, and the weight of my actions, life choices, and future felt like it was crashing down on me. "I know, Gabe. And I promise I will do everything possible to make this right. But I need your help. I need you to trust me, just a little longer."

He looked at me, his stare mixed with doubt and longing. It was as if he wanted to believe, but the fear of what had transpired was still fresh in his mind.

I moved to the corner of the room, pacing nervously, my movements hidden from view through the window. "I'm not asking you to forgive me right now," I said, my voice a plea. "I just need you to trust that I will try to fix this. Can you do that?"

Gabriel's eyes met mine, and I saw a glimmer of the boy who had looked up to me. The bond we had shared before it had all gone wrong. "I want to believe you, Tyler," he said, his voice softer now. "But you have to promise me you'll do whatever it takes to make things right."

Tears welled up in my eyes as I nodded. "I promise, Gabe. I'll do whatever it takes."

Chapter 13: Disturbing Revelation

I stood there, my heart pounding in my chest, as the police continued to shout my name from outside. Panic surged through my veins like an electric current, making it hard to think and breathe. The house walls seemed to close in on me, and my mind was a swirling mess of fear and desperation.

Gabriel, who had been scared just moments ago, suddenly looked at me with an unexpected determination. Once wide with fear, his eyes now held a glimmer of something different—something wise beyond his years. His voice quivered slightly as he spoke, "Uncle Tyler, you can't run away from this. My mum told me something: the only way you'll ever truly be free is by owning what you did and facing the consequence; this is the only way we learn."

His words hit me like a jolt. I felt a rush of emotions—shock, surprise, and a strange pride for my younger nephew. Those words sounded so much like something our mom would say. I remember her discussing the importance of owning up to our mistakes and taking responsibility for our actions.

For a moment, I was taken aback by Gabriel's maturity, his ability to see beyond the chaos and offer a sliver of clarity. I could see in his eyes that he wasn't just scared; he was genuinely concerned for me. He saw through the layers of panic and desperation and recognised the path that could lead us out of this nightmare.

As the police's demands continued to echo outside, Gabriel's words lingered in the air like a lifeline. A glimmer of hope amidst the chaos. A way out involved facing the truth, no matter how terrifying that truth might be. And in that moment, as the weight of my choices pressed down on me, I found myself nodding, a mix of fear and determination swirling within me.

Gabriel's voice resonated in my head, a reminder that I had to confront the darkness I had brought into our lives. The only way forward was through; if Gabriel could find that clarity during this turmoil, I could, too. With his words echoing in my ears, I steeled myself for what I knew I needed to do—to face the consequences of my actions and hope for a chance at redemption.

His words, so wise beyond his years, pierced through the fog of panic that had clouded my mind. At that moment, his presence felt like a lifeline, grounding me in a reality I had desperately tried to avoid.

"Gabe," my voice cracked as I spoke, raw emotion making the words tremble. "I don't know how things got to this point. I was so lost, so tangled

Chapter 13: Disturbing Revelation

up in something I thought was... I thought it was giving me purpose." Tears welled in my eyes, a mixture of shame and regret threatening to spill over. "But you're right. Your mom would've said the same thing—own up to your mistakes, face the consequences."

Gabriel's gaze held mine, a silent understanding passing between us. He wasn't just my little nephew anymore; he had become a brave inspiration and a role model, a voice of reason that I desperately needed in this chaos. With his guidance, I found the strength to take a step forward, walking alongside him toward the bedroom door and into the corridor.

As we reached the door, I paused momentarily, my hand hovering over the doorknob. The fear still lingered, the uncertainty of what awaited me outside, but I was no longer avoiding it. With Gabriel behind me, he felt like an extra backbone, and though it felt awkward relying on a ten-year-old, I needed him. I was confronting the situation head-on. Our eyes locked in that charged moment, a silent vow passed between us. We faced this together as a united front against the storm that had engulfed us.

Taking a deep breath, I proceeded down the corridor, with Gabriel still following closely behind.

Despite putting some distance from the window, the voices of the police officers became louder, their demands more urgent. My heart pounded against my chest, but I found solace in knowing I wasn't alone. Gabriel's presence beside me served as a constant reminder that I wasn't facing this challenge by myself. I understood that if there was any chance of saving my family and beginning the complicated process of righting my wrongs, I needed to confront this head-on.

 As I descended the stairs, the faint glow of lights leaked through the slight gap in the door of the front room window. My footsteps echoed in the hollow silence of the house, and my anticipation grew with each step. Gripping the doorknob, I took a moment to prepare myself, my hand hesitating over the cold metal.

 The staircase groans beneath my feet as I descend, the silence in the hallway a stark conflict with the cacophony beyond the front door. Going down, the dim glow of emergency lights penetrates the gaps around the front room door, casting an eerie hue into the corridor.

 Reaching the bottom, I stand before the closed door. Through a narrow opening, I catch sight of a

Chapter 13: Disturbing Revelation

chaotic scene—shadows moving amidst the commotion.

Standing in front of the door, it was menacing; on the other side, my future would change forever. I know that punishment awaits on the other side. It's ironic that before I open the doors, I close my eyes and pray. I never believed in God. Jenna and I grew up in a pretty non-religious house. Both our parents were lapsed Catholics, and we'd only go to church once or twice a year. Nevertheless, the handful of times I was forced to go to Sunday school will always stay in my memory. The two things I remember are the threat of going to hell and the importance of forgiveness—quite a juxtaposition in my mind.

I'm aware of the distasteful irony: praying to God after I had committed an awful crime, beating a man to what could potentially be his death. My hand trembles on the doorknob, offering both familiarity and an unknown terror.

Before stepping into this chaos, I turn to Gabriel, my voice strained with emotion. "Stay back, Gabriel," I implore, my eyes conveying the weight of the impending turmoil. "I'm sorry. Go back upstairs." In response to my plea, Gabriel, with genuine concern etched across his face, asks, "Are you going to be okay?" I give a quick nod, silently letting him know

I'll be fine. With that, I push the door open, ready for whatever's on the other side.

The front doors swing open, and I'm immediately assaulted by the blinding cascade of flashing lights from the fleet of police vehicles. It's disorienting, and for a moment, I feel like I've been thrust into a surreal nightmare. I'm temporarily blinded, struggling to make sense of the chaotic scene unfolding before me. In that doorway, fear grips me like never before, freezing me in place.

Amid the disorienting lights, the authoritative voice of the police breaks through, starting with a stern "Come forward, step away from the door frame." The words hang in the air, each repetition escalating in intensity. It's not just a command; it becomes an unrelenting drumbeat, an insistent demand that reverberates through the chaos.

In the midst of this escalating tension, Gabriel's voice reaches me from inside the house, a desperate plea echoing, "Please, Uncle Tyler, do what they say!" His words become a haunting refrain, the urgency building with every repetition. I struggle against the fear, moving forward with agonizing slowness. In response to my progress, I shout at Gabriel, my voice a mix of anger and desperation, urging him to go upstairs.

Chapter 13: Disturbing Revelation

Despite the anger, there's a poignant acknowledgement of the support in Gabriel's plea. His ten-year-old innocence becomes a beacon of solace in the midst of the chaos. Each step forward is laden with the weight of not just my own fear but the responsibility to protect the one source of unwavering innocence in this tumultuous scene. The repetition of the police commands, now more forceful and urgent, adds to the palpable tension, creating a heart-pounding symphony of fear and compliance.

My heart races, the frantic beats echoing in my ears as panic tightens its grip. The police commands persist, a relentless barrage of "Hands up in the air! Hands up in the air!" The noise is deafening and overwhelming, and I'm caught in the crossfire, trapped in a nightmarish tug-of-war of shouted orders.

The police are still shouting, their voices blending into an unintelligible commotion. They're right in front of me, and I sense Gabriel a little behind, innocent eyes witnessing a scene he shouldn't. Desperation grips me, and I find myself silently begging that he would go upstairs, shielding him from the unfolding tragedy.

But as the commands escalate to "Get on your knees!" I comply, my body moving mechanically. Tears stream down my face, and I'm weeping openly.

Amid this chaos, Gabriel, unable to bear the unfolding tragedy, runs toward me. In my panic-stricken state, I turn to face him, unintentionally making it look suspicious. The police, now concerned, react in a split second. A tragic mistake unfolds as the sound of a gunshot deafens everyone.

In that horrifying moment, reality blurs into disbelief. Gasps surround me, yet only when I turn do I grasp the full extent. My dear nephew Gabriel lies on the ground, innocence tainted by the cruel stain of blood. I scream, unable to fathom the tragic scene. The accidental shot cuts through the chaos, leaving an indelible mark of unforeseen tragedy.

Stunned by the reverberation of the gunshot, my gaze locks on the blood trickling onto the path. Every drop symbolizes the shattering of innocence, staining the ground beneath Gabriel's motionless body. I crash to the floor, the force of the impact reverberating through my body like a shockwave. Time seems to splinter, each moment stretched to an agonising eternity. The scene feels like something out of a nightmare, frozen in a suspenseful pause. The sounds around me are muffled like I'm underwater in a sea filled with all my mistakes.

As I look down at the cold, unforgiving, gravelly path, tears blur my vision, distorting the

Chapter 13: Disturbing Revelation

details into a hazy mirage. The silence is deafening, the ears still shaking from the sound of the gun, and it's as if the world is holding its breath, waiting for the inevitable collapse.

Suddenly, I'm propelled back into reality. I look up, finding myself surrounded by a looming wall of police-intimidating officers. Their uniforms blend into an indistinct fence of authority, and their shouted commands cut through the muted soundscape, slicing through the heaviness in the air.

"Get down! Stay down!" they bark, their words sharp and authoritative. With a forceful push, they drive me to the ground, my body crumpling beneath the weight of their orders. The gravel bites into my skin, and I feel the sharp edges of broken concrete beneath me. The police have succeeded in breaking not just my spirit but my physical form as well.

Lying on the floor, my body shaking with sobs, my mind is overwhelmed. Vivid images of Carlos on the floor flood my thoughts—it's like an out-of-body experience, watching myself replay the attack on him. Then, Jenna's face fills my mind, her heartbreak evident. I can feel the pain I've caused her and the irreparable damage I've done. As tears hit the pavement, my thoughts persist, and Laura enters my mind, her eyes filled with disgust and shame. I've let her down; I've let everyone down.

The Rift: A Family's Struggle with Political Extremism

The stillness of my body shatters as handcuffs click shut, their cold steel enclosing my wrists—a chilling symbol of the constraints defining my future. The police, their faces etched with stern authority and a cold detachment bordering on aggression, caution me not to move. Their voices, filled with anger, cut through the air in the thick atmosphere of despair that encases the scene. The surrounding figures, reflecting stern authority, warn me not to move. They speak to me like I'm a rat, as if they've already realised I'm no better than the rats in the sewer.

As the police dragged me up from the ground, the situation became too much to handle. I feel broken, a fractured soul unable to comprehend the magnitude of the tragedy that has unfolded. At that moment, my soul is chained by the cold reality of the handcuffs, and I am dragged along, now just a shell of the person I once was.

I go on autopilot, forced to get on my feet. My brain can't process anything, and I erupt, unable to control what I'm saying. I can't help but cry and shout apologies, the words a desperate plea for understanding in the face of the incomprehensible. After erupting, I quickly quieted down, only to erupt again, softly shouting, "It wasn't meant to happen."

Chapter 13: Disturbing Revelation

I'm dragged across the path, my vision blurred by the emergency lights, my hearing muted. I can only vaguely make out some shouting—it must have been the police calling for an ambulance mixed with panic from neighbours. My mouth tastes like gravel, and every single part of my body is hurting. The physical and emotional toll unfolds with each step, a raw and visceral experience.

Before I know it, I'm inside one of the patrol cars, the door slamming shut behind me. The metal interior feels cold and unforgiving against my skin. The noise outside is muffled, as if I'm underwater, distorting the reality of the situation.

As the car started to move, the total weight of what had just transpired crashed over me. My breath comes in ragged gasps, my chest heaving with the enormity of it all. I'm not sure where they're taking me, but at this moment, it hardly matters.

Tears stream down my face, overwhelmed by fear, regret, and sorrow. Alone with my thoughts, I can't believe the pain I've caused. In the moving patrol car, I realise my life has taken an irreversible turn, marked by this tragic mistake. Alone in the back, the consequences of my actions flood over me, drowning any rational thoughts. The pain I've caused at the rally, not just to my family but also to the family of the man brutally assaulted, blurs with the outside world as my emotions cloud my vision.

As I reflect on my actions, guilt consumes me, and the future appears uncertain. I question if freedom will be a distant memory, not only in a physical sense but also in the possibility of earning forgiveness. The concept of redemption feels daunting, particularly in not knowing if those I've wronged can find it in their hearts to forgive me.

In the midst of these concerns, I yearn to speak with Carlos' family and my sister Jenna. I wish for a chance to sincerely apologise, expressing the deep regret I now feel. My future teeters on the edge, tethered to the hope for forgiveness and the daunting possibility that I may never have the opportunity to make amends.

Chapter 15

Anguish (Jenna's Perspective)

---※---

The car's interior feels like a pressure cooker, my grip on the steering wheel tightening with every mile I race closer to home. My heart beats erratically against my chest, and my mind is a storm of shock and worry. Tyler's face in the video, with all his rage and hatred in his eyes, replays like a whirlwind of emotions threatening to consume me. I am petrified of what my brother has become, blindsided by the transformation he must have undergone over the years—an extent worse than I could have ever imagined.

I acknowledge that I let certain things slide, attempting to overlook some of his peculiar actions.

Still, now I'm haunted by the question: How did I not see it coming? I recognise that I brushed aside certain things, trying to overlook some of his peculiar behaviour. Still, now I'm haunted by the question: How did I not see it coming? The realisation hits me like an unexpected wave, and I feel so guilty; the more I reflect on the video, the more it stings. It gnaws at me, contemplating if I could have stepped in earlier to evade Tyler from the dark path he fell down.

I check that Lily and Mia have their seatbelts on. I feel numb, barely able to utter a word. I want to ask them about their time at Auntie Sarah's, but my mouth won't cooperate. An eerie silence settles in the car. My foot presses harder on the gas pedal, urging the car forward with an urgency that matches the turmoil inside me. The silence in the vehicle contrasts sharply with the chaos in my head. How could he bring that hate speech, those toxic beliefs, into my home? How could he expose his nieces and nephew to that poison? The thought ignites a fire within me, a blaze of anger burning uncontrollably.

Driving through the side streets of Pine Wood in the hope of avoiding the roadworks and getting home quicker was a mistake. The traffic around me feels like an obstacle course, a frustrating maze of cars

Chapter 15: Anguish

that refuse to move quickly enough. Trying to remain calm, my impatience rises with each passing second. Horns start to blare from all directions, a cacophony of shared frustration.

The steering wheel feels as if it might buckle under my grip. My knuckles turn white as I navigate the congested streets, propelled forward by my determination despite the obstacles. I just wanted to get home, desperate to check if Gabriel was safe. It's an awful thing to admit; he should be safe with his uncle Tyler. However, after that video of him at the rally, I didn't know what to think. The more I push, the more the universe seems to conspire against me.

As I approach another traffic light, I brake sharply, and my frustration peaks. "FUCKING HELL!" I shout, the words bursting out like water from a burst dam. The sound startles me, but it also provides a momentary release from the intense pressure building inside me.

As my voice echoes in the car, I realise how uncharacteristic that outburst is for me. I usually keep my emotions in check and find ways to stay composed even in the most challenging situations.

My impatience grows more palpable with each passing moment. In my frustration, I find myself honking the horn as if that act could magically clear the congested traffic. Uncharacteristic anger and frustration well up inside me—I just want to ensure Gabriel is okay.

As my voice echoes in the car, I realise how uncharacteristic that outburst is for me. Typically, I keep my emotions in check, finding ways to stay composed even in the most challenging situations. Then, Lily and Mia pop up in the back of the car, their innocent voices breaking through my frustration. "Are you okay, Mummy?" they ask. Their sweet tones provide a welcome distraction, and suddenly, my anger cools ever so slightly. I assure them, "I'm fine, my loves. It's just been a long day." After a moment's pause, I add, "I love you both so much."

Despite my efforts to project a strong front, I sense that Mia and Lily can pick up on something being wrong. They respond by being exceptionally sweet and well-behaved, their intuition attuned to the underlying tension. In the midst of the traffic standstill, their comforting presence becomes a silver lining amid the chaos.

At each red light, it felt like time was slipping away, making me aware of how cruel the delays were. Reflecting on today, it seemed like a whole lifetime crammed into one day—first, Gabriel's suspension, then Tyler pretending to seek redemption

Chapter 15: Anguish

but actually lying about it. I learned the true extent of my brother's actions.

At the same time, my heartfelt feelings were uncertain and scared. Each moment of waiting stretched like an eternity, and every stop became a painful break, flooding my mind with worries. The world around me turned into a series of frozen moments, like a complicated dance with fate that made the chaos and urgency even more intense.

Navigating at an agonizingly slow pace through a maze of confusing side streets, my destination was the ring road, which loops around the town of Pine Wood, offering a route to avoid those roadworks and promising a smoother journey home. However, in the current moment, a palpable sense of entrapment surrounded me.

As I manoeuvre through the intricate network of side streets, my phone incessantly buzzes in my peripheral vision. Routine news alerts dominate the notifications, with breaking events in Washington flickering across my screen through news updates. Various local news alerts about traffic disruptions fill the display, accompanied by the ever-present spam texts attempting to sell me life insurance. This ironic juxtaposition, especially after the distressing video of Tyler at the rally, intensifies the tension within the confined space of my car.

Amidst the sea of notifications, one, in particular, caught my attention—it was from Malcolm. He and his family, close friends of Matthew since our move to Pine Wood, reside on the next road. "Jenna, is everything alright on your street? I was taking Alfie [his dog] for a walk, and it looks like emergency vehicles are on your road. Hope nothing is going on with the Oswald family or dear Mrs. Prescott is okay." Living on a long cul-de-sac with various elderly couples, his concerns for the Oswalds and Mrs. Prescott made sense. Ambulances and health professionals are routinely called to the road; it's pretty much a weekly occurrence.

Despite understanding the normality of emergency vehicles on my road, my heart still sank, and worry crept in that something might be happening at home. A shiver runs down my spine, and my heart beats even faster. Trying to stay calm and rational, I avoid thinking about what could be waiting for me at home—emotional turmoil, a confrontation, or something worse. Nevertheless, with Lily and Mia in the back seat, I needed to be strong for them, pushing away the growing panic. I tell myself everything might be okay, but my mind refuses to listen.

Chapter 15: Anguish

My best efforts to remain calm were proving useless, especially as I received another couple of messages regarding the events apparently taking place on my road. Notably, the lovely elderly Connor family, residing at the opposite end of the road, expressed their concern. Conversely, some messages came from nosy neighbours like Kady, our babysitter, who mentioned passing by the entrance of our cul-de-sac. In Pine Wood, a town steeped in small-town tendencies, idle gossip is commonplace. Often, the mere presence of an emergency vehicle outside a house becomes fodder for speculation and rumours. Word in Pine Wood spreads faster than the truth. Trying to reassure myself with this knowledge, my anxiety and worry escalated to an unprecedented level, leaving me grappling with an increasingly uneasy feeling. I raced through the traffic, accelerating down the main ring road encircling Pine Wood. The atmosphere in our car was oddly quiet; Lily and Mia, with their young and compassionate hearts, tried their best to engage me and lift my spirits. Despite their efforts, I found it challenging to divert my attention. My mind remained immersed in a sea of worry and fear.

Finally making it onto the ring road, I accelerated towards home, with speed limits becoming irrelevant in my singular focus—Gabriel's safety. As I raced, I could sense the worry emanating from Mia and Lily in the back seat; they were unaware of what was unfolding. Breaking the tense silence, I shouted to the back, "Are we all okay back there?" My attempt at a small smile reflected in the rearview mirror took every ounce of energy. Both Mia and Lily affirmed they were okay, but the underlying tension persisted.

In the opposite direction, a police car came into view. The sight filled me with a sudden surge of fear, serving as a stark reminder of the chaotic circumstances that had unfolded today. The flashing lights and stern presence of law enforcement on the road intensified the knot of worry in my stomach, casting a shadow over my attempts to reassure myself and my children. The events of the day seemed to be trailing behind me, and the ominous sight of the police car only added to the sense of unease that gripped me on the journey home.

Approaching the exit road, feeling a bit better as I'm just minutes away from home, I can't help but miss Matthew's reassuring presence. I wish he hadn't gone on that business trip to Washington, not just to help with today's events involving Gabriel and Tyler but also because the area around his hotel is in lockdown due to the chaos in Capitol Hill. He's

Chapter 15: Anguish

always been my rock, the calm in the storm, knowing what to do in challenging situations. His absence magnifies my unease, and I try my best to find comfort in the thought of him beside me, guiding me through the uncertainty.

As I approached my neighbourhood, my heart raced faster. A couple of Police cars were parked along the main road, which joins onto my cul-de-sac. I looked around, feeling dazzled; there was a temporary fence patrolled by a loan officer blocking cars from accessing my road.

I made it off the slip, only needing to proceed down this main road and then take a right, which leads to my neighbourhood. As I approached, shock flashed across my face - lights were flashing, and a couple of police cars were parked along the main road, which connects to my cul-de-sac. Dazzled, I looked around, noticing a temporary fence monitored by a lone officer, preventing cars from accessing my road.

Lily and Mia both glanced to their right, asking me what was happening. Their questions became background noise as my frustration became visible. I felt lost; my house is situated in an extended cul-de-sac, offering no alternative route for a car to reach it. I decided to pull over on the main road, just a few meters from the road leading to the cul-de-sac.

Rolling down my car window, I welcomed the cool evening breeze, though it only mingled with the tension gripping my chest.

With a deep breath, I leaned out. My voice strained as I addressed the officer stationed near the roadblock. I politely waved the officer over.

"Excuse me!" The words escaped my lips, quivering with a blend of desperation and fear. "What's going on here? Is everyone alright?" The officer's countenance was solemn, his gaze fixed on the unfolding scene. "I'm sorry, ma'am, I can't divulge any information at the moment. We're still assessing the situation." I pleaded, my voice a mix of urgency and apprehension, "Do you know which house it is? Is it my little boy? Please, I need to know."

Maintaining a professionally composed demeanour while conveying empathy, the officer softly assured me, "I apologise, ma'am. I've just been assigned here to ensure only emergency vehicles can access this area. Please park your car despite the yellow lines. I'll make sure it's taken care of."

With trembling hands, I obediently parked my car as instructed. Each passing second felt like an eternity, my thoughts spinning in a vortex of anxiety and despair, leaving me alone with my tumultuous thoughts. The minutes dragged on, each one an

Chapter 15: Anguish

agonising journey into the unknown, my maternal instincts urging me to discover the truth. I just wanted to know Gabriel was safe; I just needed to know he was okay.

My mind is a whirlwind of panicked situations playing out within. What might have transpired? Is it Gabriel? Is he in danger? Panic tightens its grip on my throat, yet I mustn't let it overpower me. I even considered, could it be Tyler? Are people targeting Gabriel because of the school incident? Are they after Tyler, too? Is the video's past haunting him? My thoughts race at a breakneck pace, mirroring my uncontrollable heartbeat. I'm desperate to uncover the truth. I need to reach my house, assess the situation inside, and confront whatever nightmarish ordeal awaits me. It's as if my mind is tormenting me; this must be akin to the agony of torture.

My heart raced as I stood on the verge of abandoning my car, my instincts and fear propelling me forward. I shouted back at Lily, sternly instructing her to remain in the vehicle, my voice filled with urgency. My conscience weighed heavily on me; I didn't want to leave Mia and Lily alone in the car, but the looming danger made it a risk I couldn't afford to take. Slowing down was not an option; I had a sinking feeling that time was of the essence. The thought of leaving them behind gnawed at my soul, filling me with a profound sense of guilt and apprehension.

Me: Lily, stay in the car! Don't move, okay? Mommy needs to check something.

Lily: But Mom, what's happening? Why are there police cars?

Me: Sweetie, something is happening, but I need to find out. Just stay in the car and keep your sister safe, alright? I promise you both have nothing to worry about.

Lily: Is it about Gabe? Is he okay?

Me: (trying to reassure) I don't know, Lily. Mommy's going to find out. Just stay right here. I'll be back as soon as I can. Everything will be okay, I promise.

Lily: Okay, Mom. Please be quick.

Me: I will, sweetheart. I love you. Lock the doors and don't open them for anyone, okay?

Lily: (voice shaky) I will, Mom. Be careful.

I swiftly adjusted the heating to a comfortable level. I tuned the radio to a soft volume for Lily and Mia, ensuring their comfort before I reluctantly abandoned the car. Slamming the door shut, I stepped out and sprinted past the blockade, my heart racing.

Chapter 15: Anguish

I cast a glance past the solitary officer, adrenaline coursing through my veins, fuelled by fear and panic, urging me to press on. All I could perceive were flashing lights in the distance. I had no certainty if they were positioned outside my house or elsewhere. It felt cruel, yet a part of me held onto the hope that the incident was at someone else place. Nevertheless, with every home I sprinted past, the dread grew, knowing that it increased the likelihood that something had occurred to Gabriel or Tyler. The thought filled me with terror.

"Excuse me, please! Let me through!" I urgently called out to the innocent couple strolling with their dog. Accidentally, my elbow grazed the young woman, and she appeared startled. In contrast, the young man's expression twisted into one of annoyance as he asserted, "What the heck are you doing? "My voice trembled, and I managed a fearful "sorry." However, I couldn't afford to dwell on them at that moment. I was astounded by how utterly unaware the couple seemed of the commotion in the other direction. Amidst the blaring lights and chaotic noise, it felt as though my world was crumbling while they continued walking their dog.

As I press on down on the pavement, this seemingly endless road, my muscles throb with the strain, and my breath comes in ragged gasps.

However, I can't allow myself to slow down. Just then, my phone began to buzz, and I inexplicably halted. In my mind, I hoped it might be a message from Gabriel or Tyler, reassuring me that they were safe or sharing some mundane update to put my worries at ease.

To my devastation, it was a pointless notification informing me of what I did at the same time last year. The thumbnail cruelly depicted a photo of my whole family and me in Cancun, happy with no care in the world.

My legs ached, and breathing was a struggle. I summoned all my strength to start my journey back home. I rounded the bend and headed down the straight path leading to my house. Panic welled up within me when I noticed that all the lights near my home were distant, hinting at something amiss. My concern for Gabriel escalated, and I began talking to myself, praying it wasn't him. The flashing lights were blinding and disorientating. The loud sirens and urgent voices only heightened my unease.

As I approached my home, the sirens grew increasingly piercing, and the flashing lights seared through my vision, enveloping everything in a frantic whirl of red and blue. My heart pounded relentlessly in my chest, and anxiety knotted in my stomach.

Chapter 15: Anguish

In the midst of the chaotic scene, I discerned shadowy figures among our neighbours, standing on their front lawns with faces reflecting a blend of concern and curiosity. Some peered out from behind curtains, fixating their eyes on the unfolding events.

My house, nestled at the end of a curved cul-de-sac, remained concealed behind a curtain of emergency vehicles and flashing lights. The situation outside came into sharper focus. An ambulance and three police cars were strategically parked, intensifying my fear. Tears streamed down my face as I grappled with the terrifying unknown.

A crowd had assembled, their forms mere silhouettes in the dim, harsh glow of emergency lights. Hushed conversations and worried expressions contributed to the surreal atmosphere. The vicinity around my home was demarcated by cones and police tape, adding to the mounting sense of dread. It was as if something truly terrible had transpired, and the world had transformed into a realm of uncertainty and fear.

Approaching a cordon, my fingers clutched the hem of my coat, knuckles white with tension. Tears welled up, making it challenging to distinguish faces or details. The world around me dissolved into a vortex of colours and motion, resembling an unending nightmare from which I couldn't awaken.

The Rift: A Family's Struggle with Political Extremism

Desperately, I scoured the scene for someone to speak to, but my view remained obscured by the blinding lights, and my senses were inundated. I pressed forward, my heart pounding as I drew near the officers. "Please, let me through," I implored, my voice wavering with desperation and frustration. Panic rendered my words nearly unintelligible.

Once more, I informed the officers it was my house, and they reiterated, "It's an ongoing situation. Please stand back. This is for your safety." My gaze darted around, searching for any sign of Gabriel, of Tyler.

Desperation and fear flood my senses, and I begin to beg the officer before me, my voice cracking with each repetition. "Is it Gab? Is it Gab?" In a mantra, I keep repeating it as if saying it enough times would change the reality. The officer's expression is inscrutable, a mix of solemnity and sympathy, but they don't answer. They exchange a glance, and I can't help but feel a tightening knot of dread in my chest. The officer told me to wait a minute; he tried his best to calm me down. He called another officer who was a lot more senior to walk over.

I couldn't stay still; I felt highly agitated. Despite the officers' efforts to calm me and keep me in

Chapter 15: Anguish

place, What I witnessed was a nightmarish scene, one that seared itself into my memory. The officers, who were encircling Tyler just a few meters in front of my front door on the concrete path that divided my lawn and driveway, were acting with a sense of urgency that sent shivers down my spine. With a powerful, swift motion, they hoisted him off the ground as his cries and pleas filled the air.

His voice is raw with agony as he screams my name, 'Jenna!'" The sound of his pain hits my heart. All the anger and frustration momentarily dissipate, leaving only the unbearable weight of sadness despite knowing who the honest Tyler is—the Tyler who beat an innocent man, the Tyler spreading hate through podcasts and forums, the Tyler who infected my innocent son with his conspiracy theory cancer. Memories of a happier time when we were united as siblings flood back, accompanied by a sharp pang of nostalgia. Tyler sprawled on the floor, his hand held behind his head, frozen like a statue anchored to the ground.

My eyes shifted, and what I witnessed that night will forever haunt me, etching an indelible mark into my mind and tormenting me relentlessly. I fixated on the porch where bright red droplets of blood starkly contrasted against the pale wood, streaming down the wooden steps that led into my home. A dreadful feeling gripped my insides, and my knees weakened as I comprehended the gravity of the situation. My mind raced, attempting to unpack the scene before me, and then I saw it—Gabriel's sneakers with their soles facing upward. It was Gabriel lying on the ground, with a lone paramedic by his side. My heart felt as though it had snapped in two.

Two police officers had a tight grip on me, their voices a distant, unintelligible hum in the midst of the chaos. My desperate pleas and tears felt like they were in vain as their words got lost in the cacophony of sirens and shouting surrounding us.

In a state of utter hysteria, I called out Gabriel's name repeatedly, my voice trembling with desperation. The officers kept explaining, but their words seemed like distant whispers compared to the overwhelming fear and sorrow washing over me.

Then, another medic suddenly appeared on the scene, rushing past me directly to Gabriel. My initial heartbreak had transformed into burning anger.

I couldn't hold back my frustration, and I yelled, "Tyler, what the fuck have you done? What have you done?" Each repetition of those words was a heartbreaking cry of disbelief and horror.

Chapter 15: Anguish

Tyler, with a hopeless look on his face, continued to apologise, but he seemed burdened by the weight of his actions.

My anger surged, and the police officers had to work hard to restrain me as tears flowed freely. I found myself trapped in a whirlwind of emotions, struggling to comprehend the tragedy unfolding before my eyes. Everything around me was a blur, and my senses were overloaded. It was as if my body and soul were on autopilot, responding to the chaos that had erupted before me.

My attention was torn between Gabriel and Tyler being taken away, and a sense of desperation engulfed me. The room seemed to spin, and my legs felt weak, causing me to stumble slightly as I fought to remain on my feet. I desperately wanted to scream, but my voice caught in my throat, the words frozen within me, and time itself appeared to splinter and fracture into a million pieces, each fragment representing a shattered piece of my world.

The officers held me back, their strong grips restraining me as my chest heaved with a turbulent mix of anger and sorrow. I was desperate, trying to make sense of the chaos unfolding before my eyes. Tyler, with tears in his eyes, was led towards the back of the police car. His voice trembled as he muttered, "Sorry. I'm so sorry. Everything is my fault."

Tyler's hysterical words pierced the tension. I screamed at him, my voice heavy with anguish, "But why, Gabriel? Why him?" My question lingered, unanswered, as I wrestled with the overpowering emotions that threatened to engulf me. Tyler continued to murmur his apologies, guilt drawn across his face. "I didn't intend for any of this to occur," Tyler whispered faintly as I watched him move in the opposite direction, encircled by armed officers. If I hadn't been held back, I would have reached him; I had never felt such an intense surge of hatred coursing through my veins.

As Tyler was gently placed into the police car, I felt a profound sense of powerlessness that coursed through me like a chilling wind. The door closed with a resounding thud, sealing him inside that metal cage. It was as though the world around me had transformed into a surreal dreamscape. The streetlights cast long, eerie shadows that danced on the pavement, echoing the uncertainty and fear that had gripped my heart.

As the police car disappears into the distance, my chest heaves with sobs threatening to consume me. Released from the officers' grip, I stumble forward, my vision blurred by tears. In the periphery of my awareness, the world moves in fragments, a

Chapter 15: Anguish

disorienting dance of flashing lights and muted voices. But all I see is Gabriel lying there, fragile and broken, his life hanging in the balance.

As I crouched down, the paramedics let me sit next to him, with tears flowing down my face. Other medical personnel rushed past me, their urgent footsteps echoing in my ears. Paramedics now surround my beautiful Gabriel; their movements are swift and methodical.

Struggling for breath, I was in the grip of a full-blown panic attack. I wanted to say something. I tried to speak to my darling Gabriel and the paramedics. It was as if I had gone mute; the sight was overwhelming, and I couldn't tear my eyes away even as tears blur my vision.

"Will he be alright?" My voice quivered as I finally managed to address one of the paramedics. I repeat the question, desperately seeking the reassurance of a "he will be fine" response. Instead, I'm met with a sympathetic gaze and the words, "We're doing our best." The paramedic's further words fade into a blur, drowned out by the chaos of my thoughts. All I can focus on is the delicate nature of the situation and the fear that tightly grips me.

I sit next to him, wanting to hold his hand, but I know I'd be in the way of the paramedics. Gabriel," I whisper, my voice trembling with anxiety and torment. "Darling, are you able to hear me?" I could see him glance in my direction, a desperate attempt to utter words stifled by his voiceless struggle. "Gabriel, my darling," tears streamed down my cheeks. I had never placed faith in a higher power. Yet, internally, I prayed for my son's well-being.

With every passing second, as the paramedics work tirelessly to stabilise Gabriel, I hold onto that glimmer of hope. It drives me forward and compels me to keep fighting for my family, unity, and a world that can heal. As the world revolves around me, that hope becomes my anchor, my lifeline, in a world that has been shattered beyond recognition.

Lost in my world, I drifted deep into my cherished memories of happier times with Gabriel, if only for the briefest of moments. I just pictured his beautiful smile from earlier on in the day after our heart-to-heart, and for that split second, I felt comfort.

Back to reality, a compassionate female paramedic approached me. With a heavy heart, I rose from my contemplation, my eyes filled with an anxious plea.

The female paramedic sought to provide solace, "He's currently exhibiting a modicum of stability, and the haemorrhaging has ceased.

Chapter 15: Anguish

However, we must expedite his journey to the hospital."

Panic consumed me, prompting a relentless barrage of questions, my voice trembling with dread. "Please, can you tell me if he's going to be okay? Will he survive this? I can't lose him," I implored, my words filled with raw desperation.

The paramedic responded with gentleness and composure, maintaining eye contact to offer reassurance, "We understand your concern. The swifter we transport him to the hospital, the greater his chances of survival. Rest assured, he's in the most capable hands available. We'll do everything in our power to help him."

I nodded, knowing, please, please save him," I pleaded, my voice raw with desperation. I walked closer to Gabriel and touched his hand one last time, a silent promise that I'd do everything I could to protect him.

My heart raced as the paramedics swiftly sprang into action. They gently moved my poor little boy onto a sturdy stretcher, securing him in place. The sight of my beloved, vulnerable little boy on that stretcher shook me to the core. I watched with a mix of hope and fear as they carefully loaded him into the waiting ambulance.

The only source of comfort was the paramedics' professionalism. They worked with empathy and urgency; their experience was evident in every move they made.

As they carefully loaded my beloved son into the waiting ambulance, I stood there, my heart pounding. I felt like my entire future was hanging on by a thread. Overwhelmed by fear, I leaned down and gently kissed his forehead, my lips lingering on his pale skin momentarily.

With the paramedics getting ready to depart, my precious boy now receiving oxygen, they motion for me to join them in the ambulance. Overwhelmed with relief and anxiety, tears stream down my face as I tell them, "I'll follow you. I have Lily and Mia waiting in the car."

The paramedics, their faces filled with urgency, gently explain, "We need to go now to give Gabriel the best chance. Every second counts." Their words weigh heavily on my heart, and the guilt of leaving my other children in the car gnaws at me.

"I love you; I'll follow you," I say, my voice quivering. The thought of Gabriel being alone in that ambulance, even for a moment, feels like a dagger in my heart. My instincts as a mother are torn between

Chapter 15: Anguish

my children and the torment of this choice tears at my soul.

The ambulance roared to life, its sirens wailing and its red lights flashing in the encroaching darkness. With a sense of urgency, it pulled away from the scene, the cacophony of its emergency signals piercing the air as it vanished into the distance.

With a rush of anxiety, I hurried back to my car, worried about how long I had left Lily and Mia alone. Guilt gnawed at me for having momentarily abandoned them, even though it had been only briefly.

Once inside the car, I couldn't bring myself to give them their usual warm hugs. They sensed something was amiss. In her innocent voice, Mia inquired about what was wrong, and I replied with a quivering voice, "We just need to go and see your brother."

The drive to the Pine Wood Central Hospital was solemn, punctuated only by the heavy silence in the air. They knew something was terribly wrong, but they did their best to offer comfort with their mere presence. Their small gestures of support prevented me from plunging into a pit of despair, even though my heart was already shattered.

As I got into the car, my head and mind were a blur. The weight of the situation was overwhelming, and I desperately needed someone to talk to. I reached for my phone and dialled my dear friend, Sarah, my trembling fingers barely able to press the buttons.

"Sarah," I said, my voice quivering, "I need a huge favour. Can you please pick up Lily and Mia from the hospital? A hospital isn't the place for them, and I want to be with Gabriel right now." The guilt of passing off much of my parenting responsibilities to her today gnawed at me, but she was my closest friend, and I knew I could rely on her.

Deep down, I knew that Lily and Mia, despite their early age, could sense the gravity of the situation; they possessed emotional intelligence far beyond their years. Still, I wanted to shield them from the full extent of it, to protect their innocence as long as I could.

"Sarah," I continued, my voice laden with emotion, "I know I'll have to explain everything to you later, but right now, I'm in such a rush. I can't thank you enough for this. You're a true lifesaver. I love you, and I can't express how much your friendship means to me. You're a fantastic friend, and I promise I'll make it up to you for this. I need to be

Chapter 15: Anguish

with Gabriel, and I trust you to take care of Lily and Mia like no one else.

Sarah, understanding the urgency in my voice, didn't ask any questions. She replied, "Of course, I'll meet you there, don't worry. Just focus on Gabriel for now. I'll make sure Lily and Mia are okay."

Her words provided a small but precious reassurance during the chaos. I hurriedly thanked her once more and hung up, my foot pressing harder on the gas pedal as I raced towards the hospital, my mind consumed with worry for my little boy.

A few hours had drifted by, and the early morning light cast a pallid glow in the hospital waiting room. I had managed to steal a few moments of rest, though it was more akin to a shallow doze as my body and mind were wracked with exhaustion. Sitting there alone, the unforgiving silence of the hospital only deepened the feeling of isolation and perpetrated my anxious thoughts.

My girls, Lily and Mia, were safely ensconced at Sarah's house, a beacon of support during this tumultuous time. I couldn't have been more grateful for her unwavering friendship.

Matthew should be checking in at the airport after I had just had a conversation that weighed heavily on both of us, one of the most excruciating discussions of my life. He had rushed to the airport, and his absence left a void that was impossible to ignore.

Panic and worry relentlessly consumed me in those solitary moments. The fate of Gabriel hung in the balance, and the uncertainty was like a relentless storm. I sat there, grappling with a whirlwind of emotions that swung from seething anger at Tyler, who had a hand in this tragedy, to the profound heartbreak that clung to my heart for my ailing son.

On the TV in the waiting room, the images of the violence in the capital played. It was a significant event in the nation's history. Yet, it felt inconsequential in the shadow of my overwhelming concern for Gabriel.

Yet, there was a strange and evil irony in that room. The political chasm dividing America parallels the deep schism in my own family. Both were struggling for unity, besieged by forces tearing them apart. In a peculiar and disheartening synchrony, the division in America and the division in my own family mirrored each other, highlighting the universal struggle for harmony and understanding in times of discord.

Sitting in the waiting room, I felt like a caged animal, occasionally rising from my seat to pace around in anxious circles. It was a torturous wait,

Chapter 15: Anguish

filled with silent prayers, desperate hopes, and inner pleas for good news. If only I could turn back time and prevent Tyler from ever re-entering our lives. The regret gnawed at me, a constant reminder of the harm he had wrought upon my family.

As I sat there, my phone buzzed, and I noticed a missed call, almost certainly from Tyler in custody. I hesitated for a moment, my thumb hovering over the screen, but then I thought, "No, never again." I had promised myself that I would never speak to him, that he was no longer my brother.

Just when I thought I couldn't bear the weight of the waiting any longer, a senior consultant emerged from the depths of the hospital. He called my name, and I practically leapt to my feet. My heart raced as I fired off a million questions, hoping to glean some reassurance from his expression, but his stoic face revealed nothing. His tone, however, spoke volumes.

I'll never forget that moment. The consultant led me into a dark, still room where the doctors, their faces solemn, delivered the heartbreaking news. 'We tried our best, but I'm sorry, Gabriel is no longer with us.' The words hung heavy, the weight of loss settling in as my world crumbled.

Chapter 16

Upon Reflection (Tyler's Perspective)

---※---

The cold, unforgiving metal of the prison bars looms over me as I sit in my cramped cell, which I've called home for nine years. For nearly a decade, these prison walls have become my world. The sterile, artificial lighting casts eerie shadows on the peeling paint of the cell walls. The faint sounds of inmates shuffling down the dimly lit corridor outside are the only reminder that I'm not alone in this desolate place.

"I take a deep breath, attempting to calm the growing anxiety knotting in my stomach. Today is the day of my parole hearing, a slim opportunity to return to the world I've been absent from. The very idea of freedom should be exciting, yet it isn't. It's daunting and terrifying.

I look down at my hands, feeling the gentle moisture on my palms as I bring them together in a tight clasp. The Bible, worn and frayed from countless readings, lies on the cold metal table beside me. It has served as my sanctuary, my wellspring of strength throughout these enduring years. My spiritual journey began behind these prison walls when I had nothing but time to reflect on the choices that led me here.

I stare at the small, cracked mirror above the sink. The reflection I see is unfamiliar. The boy who used to be so sure of his rightness is gone. In his place is a man who now serves God, understanding the gravity of his mistakes and how they've affected the people he cares about.

As I adjust my prison-issued uniform, I can't help but wonder how the world has changed since I've been locked away. It's been so long since I breathed the crisp air of freedom or felt the sun's warmth on my skin for longer than an hour.

I've lost years of my life, not just within these prison walls but the time I dedicated to hate and its

Chapter 16: Upon Reflection

distribution. Most significantly, I've missed the precious moments in the lives of those I care for Jenna, my sister, and the children, Lily and Mia. They've been living without me, and I am a stranger in my family. Yet, this sentiment is overshadowed by my profound guilt regarding Gabriel. My actions have prematurely ended his life, and I bear the sole responsibility for his premature death.

It wasn't just my family life; I also wrote to Carlos' family; he had a young wife. The guilt of taking his life due to my anger will be a lifelong burden. She never responded, and it kept dredging up memories of when I lost Laura.

Today, I can start to make amends and rebuild the bridges I burned with my hatred and anger. As I sit here, waiting for my name to be called, I can't escape the fear lingering when I contemplate my family and the family of Carlos. What if they can never forgive me?

I take one last look at the Bible, clutching it tightly as a source of hope, of redemption. It's time to face the consequences of my actions and confront the past and the pain I've caused so many. Whatever happens in that parole hearing room, I know one thing for sure: I can't change the past, but I can strive to be a different man, a better man, from this day forward.

The Rift: A Family's Struggle with Political Extremism

The memories come rushing back as I sit in my prison cell, awaiting my fate. For the first four years of my sentence, I never spoke to Jenna, my sister. I would send her letters every week, pouring my heart into every word, but she never replied.

Then fate intervened most suddenly. Our father, a man I had a poor relationship with, passed away. I was allowed to attend his funeral under strict supervision. Jenna, teary-eyed and distant, stood by his casket. She looked fragile like she had aged a decade since I last saw her.

In the presence of our father's lifeless body, we finally opened the lines of communication there. Jenna, in her grief, had finally allowed me back into her world, if only with a crack.

Initially, Jenna's feelings towards me were filled with anger. Still, as time passed, I realised the consequences of my actions on her. The repercussions of that fateful night were devastating. The loss of her son, Gabriel, left her utterly shattered. Following my trial, she grappled with alcoholism and depression, seeking refuge at the bottom of a bottle. The torture of losing Gabriel and my betrayal profoundly and negatively affected her emotional well-being.

Matthew, her husband, someone I once held an intense animosity towards due to our differing

Chapter 16: Upon Reflection

beliefs, and our father, who played a pivotal role in rescuing Jenna from the depths of despair. Their unwavering support and love had served as her lifeline. Together, they founded a charitable foundation in Gabriel's name, promoting internet safety.

This initiative became Jenna's means of dealing with her grief and honouring my nephew's memory. She partially attributed my radicalisation to the internet and was resolute in her mission to create a safer online environment. She was relentless in her mission to prevent other families from experiencing the loss of a loved one due to online content. She was dedicated to ensuring that major tech companies like Google and Meta were held more accountable for the content they host.

When I look back, I can't help but feel an overwhelming sense of shame, guilt and regret. I had torn two families apart with my extremist beliefs and actions. But today, as I sit here in this cold, unforgiving cell, I have a chance to make amends. The worst thing about all this is that I can never bring back Gabriel or Carlos despite all my changes.

My name is called, breaking the grip of my memories. It's time for the parole hearing, the moment of reckoning. I look at the Bible, my source of strength, and step forward into an uncertain future.

The Rift: A Family's Struggle with Political Extremism

As I walk the corridor to the parole office, my heart pounds like a drum, each beat echoing my mixed emotions. Seeing my reflecting on one of the many mental doors, a small part of me is proud of the person I've become in prison. I've immersed myself in religion, found redemption in the words of the Bible, and worked tirelessly to improve myself. Nonetheless, that pride is dwarfed by the immense weight of guilt that hangs around my neck.

I can't help but acknowledge the irony that has defined my journey. I've traded one kind of obsession for another. Once, I was consumed by far-right ideologies and conspiracy theories that led me down a dark path that caused pain and suffering.

Now, I am immersed in a different belief system that preaches love, compassion, and forgiveness. It's a stark departure from the hate-fuelled rhetoric I once embraced. But in this transition, I've realised that the intensity of my commitment to change mirrors the fervour I once had for those destructive beliefs.

There's a certain irony in that my newfound faith in goodness and redemption has become as all-consuming as my previous descent into hatred and extremism. However, this time, I am content knowing that my path is healing, not harm. My commitment to

Chapter 16: Upon Reflection

becoming a better human to atone for my past sins gives me purpose and direction.

I want freedom from these prison walls and the guilt that gnaws at my soul daily. I like the chance to make amends for the pain and suffering I've caused, especially to Jenna. I long to prove that the person who committed those terrible acts is not who I am today.

Yet, as much as I yearn for freedom, I'm terrified of what awaits me outside these walls. The world has changed in the nine years I've been imprisoned. I've heard whispers of a society more divided and polarised than ever. A world where extremist ideologies continue to thrive and wreak havoc.

The prospect of navigating this new reality fills me with fear. I worry about whether I can resist the pull of those dark ideologies that once consumed me. Can I genuinely reintegrate into a society that may never fully accept or trust me again?

These conflicting emotions churn within me as I finally reach the door to the parole office. I take a deep breath, summoning what little courage I have left, and step inside. It's time to face my fate, lay myself bare before the judge, and hope they see the change in me and grant me the opportunity to prove that I can be a better man.

As I step into the brightly lit room, I can't help but notice the palpable tension that hangs in the air. The chamber is small and sterile, with white walls that seem to close in on me and the dull hum of fluorescent lights casting an unflattering glare on everything.

The parole board panel is an intimidating trio. The parole board sits behind a long, mahogany table; each board member is adorned with a stern determination.

The woman in the centre is impeccably dressed in a charcoal grey suit, and her steel-grey hair pulled back into a severe bun. Her gaze is piercing, her eyes cold and calculating.

To her right is a middle-aged man with salt-and-pepper hair, wearing a dark navy suit that screams authority. His posture is rigid, and he studies me with an unyielding stare.

To the woman's left, a younger man in his early thirties, his sharp jawline emphasising his seriousness. He looks as if he is barely out of law school, but his eyes tell a different story – they hold the weight of experience and judgment.

The room is flooded with a heavy silence that hangs like a dense fog, punctuated only by the occasional rustle of papers. I can hear my uneven

Chapter 16: Upon Reflection

breath, trying to steady my turbulent emotions. The stark, sterile surroundings heighten the significance of this moment.

On the table in front of each board member, there's a plain glass of water, its surface adorned with tiny, glistening beads of condensation. My reflection wavers within the droplets, a distorted reminder of the person I once was. I swallow hard. My throat dried, but I dared not reach for the water. It feels like a test, an evaluation of my self-control.

The board members remain motionless, their eyes locked onto mine, their expressions unyielding. Their gaze feels like a laser, cutting through my exterior to expose the depths of me.

I take a deep breath, feeling the weight of their scrutiny pressing down on me, and finally, I begin to speak. "Thank you for allowing me to address this board today. My name is Tyler, and I stand before you as a man who deeply regrets the choices he made in the past. The events of January 6th, 2021, will forever haunt my conscience, and I accept full responsibility for my actions on that day."

I pause, letting the weight of my words settle in the room. The panel remains stoic, their eyes locked onto me, awaiting my every utterance.

"I would like to begin by acknowledging the gravity of my crimes. I was a different person then, consumed by anger and misguided beliefs. I was lost in a world of extremism and hatred, and I allowed myself to be manipulated by those who sought to sow discord and violence. My actions that day were inexcusable, and I have carried the burden of guilt every day since."

I continue, my voice quivering with sincerity, "The hardest thing I've done during the last nine years is to forgive myself because in the Bible, it is written, 'Judge not, and you shall not be judged; condemn not, and you shall not be condemned; forgive, and you will be forgiven.' These words from Luke 6:37 have echoed in my mind as a constant reminder of the forgiveness I desperately seek."

A tear trickles down my cheek, and I quickly wipe it away. The room remains silent as I gather my thoughts.

"I have spent the past nine years reflecting on my actions, seeking redemption, and working to improve. In prison, I have found solace in the teachings of Jesus Christ. He said, 'I have not come to call the righteous but sinners to repentance.' My faith has been my guiding light, leading me towards healing and transformation."

"I comprehend that my crimes have inflicted immeasurable pain and suffering, particularly on the

Chapter 16: Upon Reflection

family of Carlos Garcia. Mere words cannot erase the anguish I've brought upon them. I carry the weight of guilt in my conscience every day. Once more, I wish to express my sincere apology.

Regarding my family – Jenna, Mia, and Lily – I cannot adequately convey the depth of my remorse for the pain I've caused you. I want you to understand that I am fully dedicated to making amends in any way possible." The silence in the room is profound, broken only by the faint sound of shuffling papers.

"As I stand before you today, I am a changed man. I have sought counselling, attended anger management classes, and dedicated myself to serving others within the prison community. I am not the same person who committed those heinous acts on that fateful day. I am humbled by the second chance at life I desperately desire."

I cast my eyes downward, feeling the weight of my plea. "I do not ask for your forgiveness lightly. I know that my crimes are of such seriousness that they have left an indelible mark on society. But I ask you to consider the transformation I have undergone, the remorse that eats at my soul every day, and the hope for a future where I can make amends."

I take one last breath, my voice quivering, and my eyes meet those of the panel, seeking some glimpse of understanding, some sign that they might see the sincerity in my words.

I'm compelled to take a seat as the board members exchange glances and scribble notes. My chair, much like the prison walls that have enclosed me for the past nine years, is hewn from unyielding stone. As I settle into this unforgiving seat, I am overcome by a profound sense of exposure and vulnerability. My thoughts drift back to that fateful day. This moment will forever haunt me, marking me with its enduring stigma.

The first vivid image that rushes into my mind is the violence I incited at the rally. I see Carlos Garcia, someone with whom I once shared a school, a man of genuine kindness and upstanding character, tragically falling to his demise, his head bleeding profusely. The memory of that instant is etched into the very core of my conscience, serving as a stark reminder of the darkness I once embraced. Then, like a cruel twist of fate, the anguished screams of Gabriel pierce through my recollections. I can hear his terrified cries and see the sheer terror in his innocent eyes as he bears witness to the chaos and violence that engulfed us. The room around me blurs as the flashback intensifies, transporting me back to that street, where anger and hatred swayed over me again.

Chapter 16: Upon Reflection

Despite my ongoing quest for redemption, these two scenes relentlessly collide in my mind. It's as though, no matter how hard I tried to forgive myself and push forward, there remains a part of me that steadfastly resists moving on.

My thoughts then turn to what Laura would think of the person I was and the person I have become. She was the love of my life, the one who perceived the goodness within me even when I was unable to see it in myself. The image of her radiant smile and her kind heart only intensifies my inner torment. I find myself pondering what judgment she might pass on the person I have transformed into, the choices I have made, and the shattered state of my life.

Tears begin to well up in my eyes, and I can't stop them. I blink furiously, trying to regain my composure. Not since my sentencing had I felt this vulnerable. The memories of that fateful day flood back with visceral intensity. I find myself transported to the courtroom, where vulnerability clung to me like a heavy shroud. The atmosphere was oppressive, and I could practically taste the tension in the air.

As I stood there, the charges were listed one by one. Manslaughter, a word I never imagined would be associated with me, echoed in my mind. It filled me with an overwhelming sense of guilt and remorse.

The gravity of my actions, the consequences of spreading dangerous information, pressed down on me. It was as though the weight of the world had settled upon me, and I couldn't escape its suffocating grip.

In the courtroom, I could feel the accusing eyes of Carlos's grieving family fixed upon me. Their silent, mournful gazes bore into my soul, a constant reminder of the pain I had caused. Justice was being served, but it was a bittersweet vindication, for no amount of punishment could ever bring Carlos back.

What struck me most that day, however, was the absence of my own family. Not a single familiar face among the spectators. It was as though that courtroom was where the old Tyler had died, and this new, remorseful Tyler was born. The isolation was as stark as the reality of my actions, and I was left to confront the consequences of my choices in a world that had turned its back on me.

In the present, the room remains intense with tension as the board members decide my fate. Their eyes bore into me, their expressions inscrutable, making my heart race. The silence feels eternal, and I'm left to grapple with the weight of my past actions.

At long last, the chair, a resolute woman in her fifties with an unwavering demeanour, shatters the

Chapter 16: Upon Reflection

heavy silence. Her voice resonates with measured authority, each word carrying the weight of profound judgment. "Mr. Tyler, your actions on that fateful day unleashed dire consequences. A young man's life was extinguished, a child left fatherless, and a wife bereft of her husband." Her unyielding gaze remains locked on me as if she's delving into the deepest recesses of my soul.

I feel a lump rise in my throat, choking back the guilt and remorse that threatens to engulf me. Each word the board member utters reminds me of the lives forever altered by my choices. I can hardly bear to imagine the pain and loss that Gabriel's family has endured.

But the chair continues, "Furthermore, your actions and the content you propagated online incited violence, with some of your followers participating in acts of terror, such as the events of the insurrection in Washington." Her words strike like a sledgehammer, and the gravity of my involvement in such events weighs heavily on my conscience.

The chairman's voice remains unyielding as she delivers the verdict. "After careful consideration, we cannot grant your parole. The crimes you committed were of such seriousness that we cannot ignore their consequences on others."

My shoulders dipped no matter how hard I attempted to maintain my composure. The verdict delivers a devastating blow, though not entirely unexpected. Securing early parole had always seemed like a distant possibility. However, the judgment provides a harsh reminder of the magnitude of my actions. As I sit in that frigid, clinical room, I'm left to ponder the lifetime sentence I've condemned myself to, not only within the confines of prison but also in the unending penitentiary of my remorse. A life sentence stretches before me, not just behind these prison walls but in the eternal prison of my guilt.

I take a deep breath, finding solace in acceptance. There's no escaping the consequences of my choices, nor should there be. I have caused immeasurable pain, a burden I must carry for the rest of my days.

Turning my attention to the board members, I offer a solemn nod of gratitude. "Thank you," I say, my voice steady, "for hearing me today and for your careful consideration." One of the board members cast a glance my way, a look filled with profound empathy. It was a silent acknowledgement of the torment I had experienced. For a moment, it offered a glimmer of understanding in the otherwise stern and unyielding proceedings.

Chapter 16: Upon Reflection

With that, I bow my head in prayer. I close my eyes and seek forgiveness from a higher power that knows the depths of my remorse, a control that can offer solace to the souls I've wronged.

As I utter my prayers, I can't help but think of the Bible verses I've clung to during my time in prison, the poems that have guided me toward redemption. I think of Jesus's teachings, love, compassion, and forgiveness. In this solemn moment, I pray that someday, my actions can be reconciled with those teachings.

The room remains silent as my prayers end, and I'm left with a profound sense of acceptance. I may never fully make amends for the pain I've caused. Still, I can spend the rest of my life seeking redemption, seeking a path toward becoming a better person, even if that path is within the confines of these prison walls. As I walk back to my cell, I'm reminded that forgiveness, if it ever comes, will be a journey, not a destination.

As I entered my dimly lit cell, my heart felt heavy, and my soul was burdened by the weight of my past. The harsh reality of my situation was a constant companion, a reminder of the mistakes I had made. Yet, amidst the darkness, I found a glimmer of hope.

Sitting on the edge of my bed, I reached for a picture of Laura on my nightstand. It was a cherished memento, a source of comfort and solace. With trembling hands, I gazed at the photo of us together and began to reflect on the moments we had shared. Her smile in the picture spoke of love and happiness, offering a glimpse of the light I longed to return to.

In that solitary moment, I resolved to embark on the long and arduous journey toward redemption, guided by the memory of Laura and the hope of making amends. With determination in my head and God now in my heart, I knew that I would find a way to redemption.

Acknowledgement

Writing this book was a journey I never saw coming, and it's my first, so that's a bit of a shocker! But I couldn't have done it without some fantastic folks.

Big shoutout to my mum and dad, Beverley and Jeffrey Krell. They took the time to read through my words and helped me make sense of it all. Their support means the world.

To my friends, thanks for sticking with me through the highs and lows of this writing gig. Your support and faith kept me going.

A special thanks to my girlfriend, who was incredibly patient throughout this process. Your support and understanding made all the difference.

And to you, the reader – yeah, you! Thanks for picking up this book. I hope you enjoy the ride.